Mallika gave him what she hoped was a sufficiently cool and professional smile.

'I'll tell you if I change my mind,' she managed, as she pulled together her scattered thoughts.

'The salary is negotiable,' Darius added, but she shook her head.

'It's not about the money,' she assured him.

Darius knew when not to push—he also knew he wasn't going to give up so easily.

'I need to go,' she said. 'Thanks for being so nice about everything.'

She put her hand out, and Darius got to his feet as he took it.

'Nice' wasn't the impression he wanted to leave her with. *'Nice'* suggested she'd forget him the minute she stepped out of the hotel. And he wasn't going to let that happen.

Dear Reader

This is my sixth book for Harlequin Mills & Boon®, and it was perhaps the most fun to write. The idea popped into my head when I was talking to a colleague who'd taken a few months off to travel around Europe. What if I had a hero who was wildly successful at what he did and had made more than enough money to fulfil his boyhood dream of spending some years just travelling around and discovering more about the world? And what if, just before he left, he met a woman who made him think that perhaps there was more to life than just living out his dream?

It took a while to get my characters just right, but Darius in the book is now exactly as I imagined him— successful, strong-willed and very, *very* attractive. Mallika is different—she's been through a lot and she's always put family ahead of anything else. As a result, while she's resilient she's also very risk-averse. She's instantly attracted to Darius but she fights the attraction, thinking that it can never work between them. Darius, however, has completely different views on the matter!

Happy reading!

Shoma

AN OFFER
SHE CAN'T REFUSE

BY
SHOMA NARAYANAN

First published in Great Britain 2014
by Mills & Boon, an imprint of Harlequin (UK) Limited,
Eton House, 18-24 Paradise Road, Richmond, Surrey, TW9 1SR

© 2014 Shoma Narayanan

ISBN: 978-0-263-24350-5

Harlequin (UK) Limited's policy is to use papers that are natural,
renewable and recyclable products and made from wood grown in
sustainable forests. The logging and manufacturing processes conform
to the legal environmental regulations of the country of origin.

Printed and bound in Great Britain
by CPI Antony Rowe, Chippenham, Wiltshire

B000 000 013 4003

Shoma Narayanan started reading Mills and Boon® romances at the age of eleven, borrowing them from neighbours and hiding them inside textbooks so that her parents didn't find out. At that time the thought of writing one herself never entered her head—she was convinced she wanted to be a teacher when she grew up. When she was a little older she decided to become an engineer instead, and took a degree in electronics and telecommunications. Then she thought a career in management was probably a better bet, and went off to do an MBA. That was a decision she never regretted, because she met the man of her dreams in the first year of business school—fifteen years later they're married with two adorable kids, whom they're raising with the same careful attention to detail that they gave their second-year project on organisational behaviour.

A couple of years ago Shoma took up writing as a hobby—after successively trying her hand at baking, sewing, knitting, crochet and patchwork—and was amazed at how much she enjoyed it. Now she works grimly at her banking job through the week, and tries to balance writing with household chores during weekends. Her family has been unfailingly supportive of her latest hobby, and are also secretly very, very relieved that they don't have to eat, wear or display the results!

Other Modern Tempted™ titles by Shoma Narayanan:

TWELVE HOURS OF TEMPTATION
THE ONE SHE WAS WARNED ABOUT

**This and other titles by Shoma Narayanan
are available in eBook format from www.millsandboon.co.uk**

To my family

CHAPTER ONE

DARIUS MISTRY WAS NOT used to taking orders from anyone. And especially not orders that came from a woman he was supposed to be interviewing. The fact that the woman had turned out to be surprisingly attractive was neither here nor there—this was strictly work, and her behaviour right now seemed more than a little strange.

'Hold my hand,' she was saying. 'Come on, she's almost here.'

Her current boss had just walked into the coffee shop, and Mallika was reacting as if it was a massive disaster. Granted, being caught by your boss while you were being interviewed for another job wasn't the best start to an interview, but it wasn't the end of the world. Mallika's expression suggested a catastrophe on a life-threatening scale—like the *Titanic* hitting the iceberg or Godzilla stomping into town.

'Please, Darius?' she said, and when he didn't react immediately she reached across the table and took his hand. 'Look into my eyes,' she pleaded.

He complied, trying not to notice how soft her skin was, and how her slim and capable-looking hand fitted perfectly into his.

'At least try to *pretend* you're my date,' she begged despairingly.

He laughed. 'You're not doing a great job either,' he pointed out. 'The whole "deer caught in headlights" look doesn't suggest you're crazy about me.'

She managed to chuckle at that, and her expression was so appealing that he sighed and put on what he hoped was a suitably infatuated look. Actually, after a second he found he was quite enjoying himself. He had a keen sense of humour, and despite his attempts to remain professional when faced with such an attractive interviewee, the situation was so completely ridiculous it was funny.

He was supposed to be evaluating Mallika for an important role in his company, and instead here he was, holding her hand and gazing deeply into her eyes. Rather beautiful eyes, actually—the momentarily helpless Bambi look was gone now, replaced with an apprehensive but intriguingly mischievous little sparkle.

'My goodness, Mallika, what a surprise!'

The woman who'd stopped by their table was middle-aged and plump and terribly overdressed. Purple silk, loads of fussy jewellery, and make-up that would have put a Bollywood item girl to shame.

'Hi, Vaishali,' Mallika looked up with a suitably friendly smile, but she didn't let go of Darius's hand.

'So this was your "urgent personal meeting", was it?' Vaishali leaned closer to Darius. 'Mallika's kept *you* a pretty closely guarded secret, I must say.'

'We...um...met recently,' Darius said, trying not to gag at the cloud of cloying perfume. It was like being smothered to death by lilies—the woman must have poured an entire bottle of perfume over herself.

'Ah, well, you deserve to have some fun,' the woman

was saying to Mallika, patting her hand in a surprisingly motherly way. 'I'll leave you with your young man, shall I? See you at work tomorrow!'

Her husband had been waiting patiently by her side, and Vaishali tucked her hand in his arm and trotted off with a final wave.

Mallika sighed in relief. 'Close shave,' she said as she released Darius's hand.

Clearly it was no longer of any use to her, but Darius felt absurdly bereft. When he'd first seen her he'd thought Mallika strikingly good-looking, in a natural, outdoorsy kind of way—not his type at all. Now, however, he found himself wishing that she'd held on to his hand just a little bit longer, and the feeling surprised him.

He wasn't entirely sure how he had lost control of the situation, and why he had not asserted himself in his usual role. He usually went for graceful, ultra-feminine women—the kind who'd learnt ballet when they were young and who dabbled in poetry in their spare time. While she was conservatively dressed, in a business suit, Mallika looked as if she'd spent her youth playing cricket with boys and beating them in every game.

Writing off his reaction to her as a momentary aberration, Darius tried to make sense of what had just happened.

'Is she that scary?' Darius asked, and when Mallika didn't answer, he prompted, 'Your boss?'

She bit her lip. 'No, she isn't,' she said after a brief pause. 'She's actually rather nice.'

He was about to ask her why she'd been so nervous, then, but he held the words back. This was a business meeting, and the fewer personal questions he asked the better. Only he didn't feel very businesslike right now.

When she'd bitten down on her lower lip his eyes had been automatically attracted to her mouth, and now he couldn't look away. Her lips were full and soft-looking and utterly feminine, and completely in contrast to her direct gaze and the firm lines of her chiselled face…

Okay, this was crazy—sitting and staring at a woman he'd met fifteen minutes ago. One whom he was supposed to be interviewing for a directorship.

'We didn't get very far with our discussion,' he said, trying to sound as if his interest in her was limited to her suitability for the role he'd been telling her about. 'There's a decent restaurant on the twenty-first floor. Would you prefer going there? Less chance your boss might pop up again.'

Mallika hesitated. It had seemed so glamorous when someone from the Nidas Group had headhunted her to discuss a director level role. Nidas was big—it had been set up by a bunch of young dotcom entrepreneurs a decade ago, and they'd struck gold in almost every business they'd tried their hand at.

They'd started off with online share trading and investments, but later branched off into venture capital and real estate and done much better than players who'd been in the market for thrice the time. Being considered for a directorship in the firm at the age of twenty-nine was a huge ego-boost—it wouldn't have been possible in any other firm, but at Nidas the directors were quite young, and they didn't hold her age against her.

Her first few meetings with Nidas had been preliminary ones, screening her for this final interview with Darius Mistry. For a few days she'd actually thought she could do it—be like any of the other women she'd gone to business school with, take charge of her career, interview with other employers, pretend that she had a *normal* life like everyone else. Reality was sinking in only now.

She glanced across at Darius. When she'd heard the name she'd imagined a paunchy, cheerful, white-haired man—she'd had a Parsi drama teacher at school who'd also been called Darius, and he'd looked just like Santa Claus minus the beard. Darius Mistry had come as a bit of a surprise.

True, his Persian ancestry showed in his pale colouring and hawklike features, but he was in his early thirties, tall and broad-shouldered, and as unlike her former drama teacher as an eagle from a turkey. Not good-looking in the traditional sense, more disturbingly attractive, and he emanated a quiet power and control that had Mallika caught in its glow.

He was still waiting for her to answer, she realised. 'No, I'm fine here,' she said. 'Actually, I just made up my mind. I don't think I want to take the interview any further. I'm sorry—I should have thought this through properly.'

Darius frowned. This afternoon really was *not* going to plan. Mallika had been interviewed by his HR team, as well as by one of his colleagues, and everyone who'd met her had been very impressed. Apparently she'd come across as being sharply intelligent and very, very good at what she did. He'd also looked at the performance of the real estate fund she managed. It had done extremely well, even in a volatile and completely unpredictable market, and before he'd met Mallika he'd built up an image of a hard-nosed, practical businesswoman.

The reality was different enough to be intriguing.

For a few seconds he wondered if she was playing hard to get. People used all kinds of techniques to drive up the benefits package they were offered, but very few started so early in the process. And Mallika looked troubled, a little upset—whatever the reason for her sudden decision to stop the interview process, it definitely wasn't a hard-nosed or practical one.

'You've spent almost five years with your current firm,' he said. 'I know the thought of switching jobs can be a bit overwhelming, but there's no harm going through with the interview process, is there? Once you hear what we're offering you can always say no.'

'I guess…' she said slowly. 'I just don't want to waste your time.'

'My whole night is dedicated to you,' he said.

Promptly Mallika thought of all the things they could get up to together. Her cheeks flushed a little and she took a hasty sip of water, hoping he hadn't noticed her confusion.

'So, how much has Venkat told you about the job?' Darius asked.

'He told me about how you and he set up the share trading division,' she said. 'And how you got a real estate fund going, and that you now want to concentrate on the venture capital side and hire someone to manage the fund for you.'

'That's right,' Darius said. 'The fund was an offshoot of our investments business and it's been doing well—we've consistently outperformed the market.'

She seemed interested, Darius noted as he began telling her more about the role. She was frowning in concentration, and the few questions she asked were focussed and showed that she'd done a good deal of research on the firm and on the job. He asked a few questions in turn, and it was clear that Venkat hadn't been wrong. Mallika knew pretty much everything there was to know about running a real estate fund.

'Does it sound like something you'd like to do?' he asked finally.

It was as if he'd shaken her out of a daydream—her vibrantly alive expression dulled, and her shoulders slumped just a little.

'I love the sound of the job,' she said, almost unwillingly. 'But the timing's not right for me. I have a lot going on right now, and I think maybe it's best I stay where I am.'

'Do you want to take a day to think it over?'

Mallika shook her head. 'No, I...I think I'm pretty clear that it won't work out. I'm so sorry—I know you have a busy schedule, and I should have thought this through properly before agreeing to meet you.'

She looked so genuinely contrite that he impulsively leaned across the table to cover her hand with his, making her look up in surprise.

'Don't worry about it,' he said, masking his disappointment. 'I'm meeting other people as well, but if you do change your mind let me know.'

Mallika blinked at him, uncharacteristically at a loss for words. It was like being hit by a train, she thought, confused. She'd been so focussed on what he was saying, on trying to stay professional, that she'd forgotten quite how attractive he was. Then he'd smiled and taken her hand, and the feel of his warm skin against hers had sent her long-dormant hormones into overdrive.

We like this man, they were saying excitedly. *Where did you find him? Can we keep him? Please?*

So much for a dispassionate admiration of his looks, she thought, trying to quell the seriously crazy thoughts racing through her brain. There was good-looking, and there was scorching hot—and Darius definitely fell into the second category. The first time she'd grabbed his hand she'd been too worked up to notice—this time a simple touch had sent her hormones into overdrive.

Gingerly, she slid her hand out from under his and gave him what she hoped was a sufficiently cool and professional smile.

'I'll tell you if I change my mind,' she managed as she pulled together her scattered thoughts.

'The salary is negotiable,' he added.

She shook her head. 'It's not about the money,' she assured him. 'But thanks for letting me know.'

Darius knew when not to push—and he also knew he wasn't going to give up so easily.

Mallika looked as if she was all set to leave, and he glanced at his watch. 'It's almost eight-thirty,' he said. 'I'm starving, and I'm sure you are too. D'you have time for a quick bite?'

Perhaps he could get to the bottom of her sudden withdrawal and convince her otherwise.

He was almost sure she was going to say yes, but then her phone pinged and she gave the display a harassed look.

'I need to go,' she said, her attention clearly torn between him and whoever had just messaged her. Her expression was distracted as she stood up hurriedly, her short curls swinging around her cheeks. 'Thanks for being so nice about everything.'

She put her hand out, and Darius got to his feet as he took it. 'Nice' wasn't the impression he wanted to leave her with. 'Nice' suggested she'd forget him the minute she stepped out of the hotel. And he wasn't going to let *that* happen.

'I'll be in touch,' he said, keeping her hand in his a fraction longer than strictly necessary.

She didn't reply, but she blinked once, and he realised that she wasn't quite as unaffected by him as she was pretending to be. It was a cheering thought, and he smiled as she walked away.

He'd found her intriguing—an unusual mix of the ultra-competent and the overcautious. And the attraction between them had been hot and instantaneous—if it hadn't been a work meeting he would definitely have taken things further. As it was, he was forced to let her walk away with only a tepid assurance of being in touch later.

The smell of freshly baked bread wafted past, reminding Darius of how hungry he was. He glanced around. Eating alone had never appealed to him, and if he stayed Mallika's boss might see him and come across to ask where Mallika was. He felt strangely protective of the intriguing woman he had only known for a couple of hours.

Mentally he ran through his options. Going home and ordering in. Calling up a friend and heading to a restaurant. Turning up at the excruciatingly boring corporate event he'd earlier declined.

The corporate event was the least appealing, but it would give him an opportunity to network with a bunch of people who could be useful to Nidas in the future. It wasn't too far away, either, and if he left now he'd be able to get there, hang around for an hour or so and still get home in time to catch the last bulletin on his favourite news channel.

He was handing the attendant his valet parking ticket when he spotted Mallika getting into an expensive-looking chauffeur-driven car. She was talking on the phone, and he caught a few words before the doorman closed the door for her and the car zoomed off.

'I'll be home in twenty minutes,' she was saying. 'I *told* you I had a meeting, Aryan. No, I haven't decided. I'll talk to you later…'

Whoever Aryan was, he sounded like a possessive control freak. Darius frowned. He hadn't asked Mallika, but he could have sworn she wasn't married. No *mangalsutra* necklace or rings—but lots of married women didn't wear those. And the way she'd looked at him for that one instant…

Darius shook himself. He was rarely wrong about these things, but meeting Mallika seemed to have seriously addled his brains. He was missing the obvious. She'd hardly have asked him to pretend to be her date if her boss knew that she had a husband.

Restored to his normal confidence once he'd figured that out, he tipped the valet parking attendant lavishly as he got into his car. Not married, and probably not in a serious relationship either. Hopefully this Aryan was her interior decorator, or her tax advisor, or someone equally inconsequential.

'What d'you mean, she wasn't interested?'

'She doesn't want to change jobs,' Darius explained patiently.

He and Venkat had joined the Nidas Group on the same day, and had spent the last decade setting up the businesses they now headed. Darius was the stable, intelligent one—the brains behind most of what they'd achieved together. Venkat was a typical sales guy—competitive, pushy, and notoriously impatient. Outside of work he and Darius were close personal friends, but right now Venkat's expression was that of a bulldog being asked to let go of a particularly juicy bone.

'*Why* does she not want to change jobs? Did you tell her how much we're willing to pay?'

'I did,' Darius said. 'She said she doesn't need the money.'

'You need to meet her again,' Venkat said flatly. 'I have absolutely no clue about this fund management stuff, and if you're leaving we'll go under before you know it. This girl's really good, and she seemed keen until she met you. I'd have thought it would be the exact opposite—girls usually fall for you on first sight. What in heaven's name did you do to put her off?'

'Told her that she'd be working with a bunch of total scumbags,' Darius said, deadpan. 'Look, I'm not prepared to let her go, either, but it will be better to give her some time to think things over and change her mind. I'll make it happen. But in the meantime I've got a bunch of other CVs from HR. Some of them with equally impressive track records.'

Venkat grunted. 'I'll go through the CVs, but you need to work your magic with this girl. Otherwise you can jolly well put your exciting plans on hold and stay here until you can find someone to replace you. I'm terrible at all this HR sort of stuff—you're the one who gets everyone eating out of your hand. Make this Mallika an offer she can't refuse.'

Darius bit back a sigh. Once Venkat decided he

wanted something he was like an unstoppable force of nature.

'I'm a businessman, not a Mafia don,' he said drily. 'Let me do it my way. I have an idea on how to win her...'

CHAPTER TWO

THE FLAT WAS DARK when Mallika let herself in, and she felt a familiar pang of loss as she put the lights on and surveyed the empty living room. Nothing was the same without her parents, and having a brother who'd completely retreated into his shell emphasised her loneliness rather than reduced it.

It had been a gruelling week. Her job involved meeting builders and visiting construction sites and then spending hours hunched over her computer, calculating the possible return she'd get from each investment she made for her fund.

The Mumbai property market had been at its volatile best these last few months, and investors were wary. Which meant that there was a risk of projects stalling—which in turn meant that buyers who'd already invested found themselves with large amounts of capital locked up and no hope of returns in the short term. And the fund that Mallika worked for was seriously considering stopping investment in properties that were under construction.

The kitchen was dark as well. The cook would have gone home some hours ago, leaving dinner out in microwaveable dishes for Mallika and Aryan. She wasn't particularly hungry, but dinner was the only meal she could make sure her brother actually ate.

The lights in his room were on, and she knocked before entering.

'Aryan? Dinner?' she asked, her heart twisting as she watched him hunch over his laptop. It was as if he didn't see the world around him any more, finding reality in the flickering screen of his computer instead.

'In a minute,' he said, not even looking up.

'Did you have lunch?' she asked, and he shrugged.

'Lalita gave me something,' he said. 'You go ahead and eat—you must be tired.'

It was a measure of how little she expected from him that she actually felt pleased he'd realised how exhausted she was. Leaving him to his computer, she went back to the kitchen—she'd make sure he had something to eat later.

For the last couple of days she'd not been able to get Darius out of her head. The way he'd looked at her, his smile, his voice—it felt as if she'd spent hours with him rather than just a few minutes.

He'd said he'd be in touch, but two days had gone by and he hadn't called. Maybe he'd found someone else more suitable for the role. Someone who *didn't* spot their boss and freak out halfway through a discussion, or run out on him without warning.

Idly she opened the contact list in her phone and stated scrolling down it. Darius Mistry. She had his mobile number and his email ID, and the temptation to drop him a text or a short email was huge. She could apologise once again for running out on him. Or tell him that she'd changed her mind about the job.

When it came to professional communications she

was confident and practical, but somehow with Darius she found herself prevaricating. Her shyness prevented her from getting in touch for anything other than strictly business reasons.

She was still mulling things over when her phone rang, and she almost dropped it in surprise.

'I was just thinking about you,' she blurted out, and then blushed furiously. Darius was probably already convinced of her weirdness—she didn't need to make it worse. 'I mean…I was just thinking over what you said about this being the right stage in my career to change jobs…'

'Reconsidering, I hope?' he said smoothly, and went on without waiting for her to answer. 'Look, I know you've said you're not interested, but I've interviewed around a dozen completely unsuitable people and I'd really like a chance to pitch the job to you again. Preferably in a place where your boss isn't likely to land up and ruin my sales pitch.'

One part of her felt disappointed that he hadn't called just to speak to her, but she shook herself crossly. *Of course* his interest in her was purely professional. What had got into her?

'I'm really not interested in changing jobs, Darius,' she said, firmly suppressing the little voice in her head that told her to go and meet him anyway. 'And I've wasted your time once already—I wouldn't want to do it again.'

Darius briefly considered telling Mallika that time spent with her would definitely not be wasted, but he bit the words back. This wasn't a seduction, and he'd already made it clear that when it came to business he was as determined as she to get what he wanted.

'It's part of my job,' he said lightly. 'Even if you don't want to join us now, at least I'll get to tell you about the company—and who knows? Maybe you'll want to join at some later time.'

'All right, then,' Mallika conceded. 'When shall I meet you?'

'Tomorrow,' he said decisively. 'Lunch at one of the restaurants in Lower Parel? That's nearer my office than yours, and hopefully we won't run into anyone you know.'

Darius was beginning to wonder if he'd been stood up when Mallika finally walked into the restaurant. The first thing that struck him was that there was a strained expression in her lovely eyes. The second was that she looked anything but tomboyish now.

Granted, her hair was still styled for convenience rather than glamour, and her make-up was kept to the bare minimum. But she was wearing a sari today—a dark blue silk affair, with a muted print—and her figure was spectacular in it. And her spontaneous smile when she saw him was the best welcome he could ever have hoped for.

He stood as she walked up to him, and Mallika began to feel ridiculously nervous. It was a Friday and he was dressed casually, in a white open-necked cotton shirt over jeans. His thick hair looked slightly damp from the shower, and she had a second's insane urge to reach up and run her fingers through it.

To cover her confusion she held out her hand, and he took it, briefly clasping it between both his hands before he let go.

'Hi,' she said. 'I'm not too late, am I?'

He shook his head. That smile had lit up her face, but now the worried expression was back in her eyes.

'Is everything okay?' he asked quietly once they were both seated and the waiter had put their menu cards in front of them and retired to a safe distance.

Her eyes flew up to his. 'Yes, of course,' she said, sounding just a little defensive.

Aryan was going through a particularly problematic phase, and in the normal course of things she wouldn't have left him alone at home. But she'd promised Darius, and there were meetings in the office that she couldn't avoid. Just this once Aryan would have to manage on his own, with just Lalita the cook to check on him.

'You look tense,' he said. 'Like you're trying to remember whether you locked your front door when you left. Don't worry about it—burglars are usually deeply suspicious of open doors. If it's unlocked, there's absolutely no chance of a break-in.'

She laughed at that. 'What if I did lock it?'

'Ah, then I hope you have a good security system.'

'A simple lock, and a brother who won't notice if someone puts every single thing in the house into packing cases and carries them away under his nose. As long as they don't touch his computer.'

He smiled, his eyes crinkling up at the corners in a maddeningly attractive way. 'Sounds like my kind of guy. Younger brother?'

Mallika nodded. She hardly ever mentioned Aryan in casual conversation, and the ease with which the reference had slipped out surprised her. Darius was beguilingly easy to talk to—she'd need to be on her guard a little.

The waiter was hovering behind her, and she turned her attention to the menu.

'The fish is good,' Darius said.

'It looks delicious,' Mallika said, glancing at the next table, where another waiter had just deposited two plates of grilled fish. 'I'm vegetarian, though.'

'Then the gnocchi?' he said. 'Or the spaghetti in pesto sauce?'

Mallika finally chose the spaghetti, and a glass of wine to go with it—Darius, who'd never paid good money for a vegetarian meal before in his life, found himself ordering grilled vegetables and pasta. A lot of strict vegetarians were put off by someone eating meat at the same table, and he definitely didn't want to risk that. He was on a charm offensive today, and determined to win her over.

'How's your boss?' he asked.

'She's miffed I didn't tell her I was dating someone,' Mallika said with a sigh. Vaishali was a lovely person, but the concept of personal space was completely alien to her. 'She wanted to invite both of us to her house for dinner—I had a devil of a time wriggling out of that one.'

'What did you say to her?' Darius asked, unable to keep a glint out of his eye.

'That I'd been wrong about you and you were actually really self-centred,' Mallika said, delighted she'd managed to keep a poker face. 'And possessive—and controlling.'

She sounded remarkably cheerful about it, and Darius's lips twitched.

'So we aren't dating any longer?'

'We are,' Mallika said. 'You have a few redeeming qualities, but I'm not as sure about you as I was. We're dating, but I'm not introducing you to friends and family just yet.'

'Wouldn't it have been easier to remove me from the scene altogether?'

'If I'd written you off she'd have tried setting me up with a perfectly horrible second cousin of hers. She's spent the last two years trying to palm him off on every unmarried woman she knows.'

'Maybe he's not so bad?' Darius suggested carefully. 'You should meet him—keep your options open.'

Mallika shuddered. 'No, thanks. I've met him once, and that was once too often. He spent forty-five minutes telling me how rich he is, and how he made his money. And he breathes really heavily.'

'Hmm…'

Darius's eyes were dancing wickedly, and Mallika felt a little jolt of awareness go through her. It had been so long since she'd spent any time with an attractive man that she was ridiculously susceptible.

'Can I ask you something?'

She gave him a wary look. 'Yes.'

'Are you atoning for the sins of a past life by working for Vaishali?'

'She's been very good to me,' Mallika said stiltedly, and when he raised an eyebrow she went on in a rush. 'No, really. She can be a bit overpowering at times, but I owe her a lot. I didn't mean to make her sound like a nightmare boss.'

She sounded as if it really mattered, and Darius nodded.

'If you say so.' He was silent for a few seconds as the waiter put their drinks in front of them. 'So, should I tell you a bit more about the job and the company? You can make up your mind then.'

She nodded, and listened carefully as he explained again about the company structure and the role that he was offering. Unlike her current company, which invested solely in real estate, the Nidas Group had evolved into a conglomerate of companies that included a brokering house, a consumer lending company and the fund where Darius was offering her a job. Darius himself was moving on—he didn't give her any details, but she assumed it was to head up a new division—and he didn't have enough capacity to manage the fund as well.

'I have a question,' she said, once he'd finished telling her about the job. 'Why do you think I'm right for the position?'

'You have a superb track record,' Darius said. 'And Venkat was very impressed after he interviewed you.'

'But *you* haven't interviewed me,' she pointed out. 'Or do you trust Venkat that much?'

'I have every intention of interviewing you,' Darius said, his brows quirking. 'The second you tell me that you're actually interested in the job I'll start firing questions at you.'

Mallika stared at him for a few seconds, and then burst out laughing.

'You have a point,' she said. 'So—the job sounds perfect. It's the logical next step in my career and like you said, I've been in my current job for five years and I'm beginning to stagnate.'

'I can see a "but" coming,' he murmured.

'Yes… I mean…'

'It's not convenient from a personal point of view?' Darius supplied when she hesitated.

Mallika nodded. 'That's it. I can't tell you the details, but...'

'I don't need to know the details,' Darius said. 'But if you tell me what exactly it is that your current company is doing to help you maybe I can see if we can work something out.'

Darius could smell victory, and he wasn't about to let this one go.

'I don't have fixed hours,' she said in a rush. 'Some days I reach work at eight, and some days I go in only in the afternoon. And I do site visits on my own when it's convenient to me. Sometimes I work from home, and there are days when I'm not able to work at all.'

She ground to a halt, her eyes wide and a little apprehensive. Clearly whatever was happening on the personal front was very important to her. He wondered what it was. The kind of flexibility she needed was normally required only if an employee had to care for a sick child or an elderly parent. Mallika wasn't married, and from what she'd said her younger brother sounded responsible. A parent, then, he decided.

The unwelcome thought that she might be going through a messy divorce came to mind, but he pushed it away. A divorce might need her to take time off work, but it wouldn't need her to work from home. It was far more likely that one of her parents needed to be cared for.

He thought for a while. 'We might be able to let you do the same,' he said slowly. 'Can I work this out and get back to you?'

'But when I asked Venkat he said you don't have a flexible working policy!' she said.

'It hasn't been formally approved yet,' Darius said. 'We're still working on it. Yours could be a test case.'

Their food had arrived, and Mallika took a bite of her spaghetti before answering. 'You know,' she said conversationally, 'the job market's really bad nowadays.'

'It is,' Darius agreed, frowning a little.

'And bonuses are dropping and people are getting fired every day.'

'Yes.'

'So you could probably hire anyone you wanted, right? With just as much experience and no complicated conditions. Why are you still trying to convince *me* to take the job?'

When it came to work, Mallika was sharp and to the point. She was intelligent—obviously she was, or Venkat wouldn't have considered hiring her. But Darius found himself wondering why exactly he *was* trying so hard to convince her. He'd never tried to recruit an unwilling candidate before—he'd never had to. And while she was definitely his first choice for the job, there were at least two others who could do the job equally well.

Had this just become about winning? Or perhaps he hadn't been thinking clearly since taking her hand in that coffee shop several days ago. What was going on?

'Venkat's interviewed pretty much everyone in the industry,' he said. 'You're the best fit for the role.'

'But the second best might end up doing a better job,' she said. 'He or she'd be more inclined to take the offer to begin with.'

'It's not just about technical skills,' Darius said. 'We think you'd adjust well to the organisation's culture. And we also need to improve the firm's diversity ratio, now that we're likely to get some foreign investment into the company. That's one of the things investors are likely to look at. There are a lot of women at junior levels, but very few at middle or senior management. There weren't too many CVs that fitted the bill *and* belonged to women—and other than you none of them made a decent showing at interview.'

'But I'm sure you have male candidates who're suitable,' she said, her brow wrinkling. 'Surely this diversity thing isn't so important that you've not interviewed men at all?'

'Venkat's interviewed quite a few,' Darius said. 'Apparently you did better than them as well. Diversity's not more important than talent—it's just that now we've found you we don't want to let you go.'

His gaze was direct and unwavering, and Mallika felt herself melting under it. The attraction she'd felt the first time she'd met him was back in full force—if he told her that he wanted her to join a cult that ate nuts and lived in trees she'd probably consider it seriously. Shifting jobs was a no-brainer in comparison—especially when he was guaranteeing a higher salary and no change to her timings.

She was about to tell him that she'd join when a shadow fell across their table.

'Darius!' a delighted male voice said. 'It's been years, my boy—how are you?'

The speaker was a stalwart-looking man in his early forties, who beamed all over his face as he clapped Darius on his shoulder. The blow would have pitched a weaker man face-down into his grilled vegetables, but Darius hardly winced.

'Gautam,' he said, standing up and taking the man's hand in a firm grip. 'Long while... I didn't know you were back in Mumbai.'

'Just here for a visit. And…? You're married and everything now? Is this the new Mrs Mistry?'

He looked as if he was about to clap Mallika on the shoulder as well, and Darius intervened hastily.

'No, Mallika is…a friend.'

'Aha! A Miss Mystery, then, not a Mrs Mistry—is that right?' Clearly delighted at his own wit, Gautam smiled even more broadly. 'I'll leave you to it, then. Catch you online later—I'm in Mumbai for a week more…we should try and meet.'

'Yes, I'll look forward to that.'

Darius waited till the man had moved away before sitting down, shaking his head.

'It's fate,' he said solemnly. 'Last time it was your boss—this time it was Gautam. We can't meet without running into someone we know.'

Mallika chuckled. 'He seemed a cheerful guy. He reminds me of a story I read as a kid—there was a man who smiled so wide that the smile met at the back of his face and the top of his head fell off.'

'That's such an awful story,' Darius said. 'Were you a bloodthirsty kind of kid?'

'I was a bit of a tomboy,' she said, confirming Darius's first opinion of her. 'Not bloodthirsty, though.'

She frowned at her plate as she chased the last strand of spaghetti around it. Finally managing to nab it, she raised her fork to her mouth. The spaghetti promptly slithered off and landed on her lap.

'And *that's* why my good clothes never last,' she said, giving the mark on her sari a resigned look as she picked up the pasta and deposited it back on her plate. 'I'm as clumsy as a hippopotamus.'

Anything less hippopotamus-like would be hard to

find, Darius thought as he watched her dab ineffectually at the stain with a starched table napkin. Her curly hair fell forward to obscure her face, and her *pallu* slipped off her slim shoulder to reveal a low-cut blouse and more than a hint of cleavage.

Darius averted his eyes hastily—looking down a girl's blouse was something he should have outgrown in high school. The one glimpse he'd got, however, was enough to make him shift uncomfortably in his chair. Really, Darius was so off-kilter he could hardly understand the effect she was having on him.

'Here, let me help with that,' he said, after Mallika had dropped the napkin twice and narrowly missed tipping her plate over. He got up and, taking a handkerchief out of his pocket, wet the corner in a glass of water and came to her side of the table to attend to the sari.

Mallika went very still. He wasn't touching her—he was holding the stained section of sari away from her body and efficiently getting rid of the stain with the damp handkerchief. But he was close enough for her to inhale the scent of clean male skin and she had to fold her hands tightly in her lap to stop herself from involuntarily reaching out and touching him.

'Thanks,' she said stiltedly once he was done.

'You're welcome.' Darius inclined his head slightly as he went back to his side of the table. 'Dessert?'

'I should choose something that matches the sari,' she said ruefully as she recovered her poise. 'I love chocolate, but I'm not sure I dare!'

'Blueberry cheesecake?' he asked, his eyes dancing with amusement again. 'Or should we live life dangerously and order the sizzling brownie with ice cream?'

'The brownie, I think...' she started to say, but just

then her phone rang, and her face went tense as she looked at the display. 'I'm sorry—I'll need to take this call,' she said.

'Haan mausiji,' he heard her say, and then, *'Ji. Ji. Nahin,* I had some work so I had to go out. Calm down... don't panic. I can get home in ten minutes—fifteen at the most, depending on the traffic.'

Her face was a picture of guilt and worry as she closed the call, and his heart went out to her.

'I'm sorry,' she said. 'I need to go. It was a lovely lunch, and thank you so much for putting up with me. I'm really sorry about rushing off again...'

'Don't worry about it,' he said gently. 'Do you need a lift anywhere?'

She shook her head. 'I have a car. Is it okay if I go now? I hate leaving you like this, but I really do need to get home as soon as possible.'

'It's not a problem at all,' he said. 'Take care, and we'll talk soon.'

He put enough money on the table to cover the bill plus a hefty tip, and walked her to the door of the restaurant. Her driver took a couple of minutes to bring the car round, and Mallika was clearly on tenterhooks until he arrived.

'Bye,' she said as the car pulled up and she slid into the back seat. 'I'm really, really sorry about this.'

She clasped his hand impulsively before she closed the car door, and Darius was left with the feel of soft, smooth skin on his. The subtle fragrance of her perfume hung in the air for a few seconds after she left.

He gave himself a shake before turning away to walk back to his office. This was not the way he'd planned to end their meal. He'd sensed she was on the point of accepting the role when they'd been interrupted and he could not be more frustrated with his lack of success so far. But it wasn't over—not when he was this close to getting what he wanted.

CHAPTER THREE

'WELCOME TO NIDAS,' Venkat said, giving Mallika a broad smile. 'I'm so happy you finally decided to join.'

'Same here,' Mallika said cautiously as she shook his outstretched hand.

All the old doubts about changing jobs had come flooding back now that she'd actually done the deed. She'd told Vaishali about the job the day after she'd met Darius, feeling like a complete traitor. But Vaishali had been surprisingly nice about the whole thing. Apparently she had been toying with the idea of taking a sabbatical herself, and she wasn't sure if Mallika's flexible working hours would be acceptable to her replacement.

Feeling a bit like a fledgling, shoved out of its nest before it could fly, Mallika had emailed Darius, confirming that she'd be able to join Nidas in a month. He'd been travelling, and someone from his HR team had got in touch to figure out her salary structure and joining date. Darius hadn't even called her, and Mallika couldn't help feeling a little upset about it. And now that she was actually part of Nidas and about to start work, she was very nervous.

The sight of Venkat wasn't exactly inspiring either.

Short and squat and rather belligerent-looking, Venkat was as different from her previous boss as possible.

'We've set up an orientation for you with the team,' he was saying now as he ushered her into his room.

'Darius told me—' Mallika began, but Venkat interrupted before she could complete her sentence.

'Oh, Darius is a busy chap—he won't be able to take you through everything himself.' He peered at her owlishly. 'You do know he's moving out of the firm, right?'

Mallika drew in a sharp breath. A lot of things were suddenly falling into place. Darius's insistence that she join as soon as she possibly could. His asking Venkat to set up her induction plan instead of doing it himself. The lengthy meetings with the other directors, ostensibly to help her get to know them before she joined.

A black curl of disappointment started up in the pit of her stomach. He'd had multiple opportunities to tell her and he'd consciously decided not to. It felt like a betrayal, unreasonable though that was. Unconsciously, a large part of her decision to take the job had been based on the assumption that Darius would be around and that she'd be working closely with him.

Serve her right—trusting a man she hardly knew, she thought, squaring her shoulders and doing her best to keep Venkat from noticing how upset she was.

'He didn't tell me that he was moving out altogether,' she said crisply. 'Though I did get the impression that he'd be cutting off from this part of the business in a month or so.' She was determined to cover her disappointment with cool professionalism.

'Even less, if he has his way,' Venkat said, and an expression of bewildered loss crossed his face for an instant. 'It was a shock when he told me. We've worked

together for years—we set up this business together—
and out of the blue he tells me he's quitting. I still don't
understand why he's doing it.'

Strongly tempted to find out more, Mallika bit down
on her questions. It shouldn't matter to her where Darius
was going or why.

'When you interviewed me *you* didn't mention that
Darius was leaving the firm,' she reminded Venkat.
'Why did you assume I'd know now?'

He had the grace to look embarrassed. 'I couldn't
tell you before you joined,' he said. 'Darius is a pretty
big shareholder, and the news of his leaving isn't public
yet. I thought he might have told you since—I got the
impression you guys are pretty friendly.'

He took in Mallika's suddenly stormy expression and
changed the subject in a hurry. 'Now, I thought I'd first
introduce you to some of the key people in your team,
and then you can start going through our current investment strategies. The team's brilliant—I've been working with them pretty closely for the last few months. I've
put them on to a few good things as well. Of course now
you're here you'll be in full control, but you can reach
out to me whenever you want.'

As the day went by Mallika found herself feeling more
and more confident. Venkat evidently valued her input,
and his style of working wasn't as different from hers
as she had feared.

She was packing up for the day when there was a
knock on the door of her room. Assuming that it was
the overzealous tea boy, who'd been popping up every
half an hour, she said, 'Come in!' and continued stuff-
ing files into her laptop bag.

It was a few seconds before she realised that the man in the room was about twice as large as the tea boy.

'Darius!' she said, her brows coming together in an involuntary frown as she saw him. 'I was wondering if I'd see you today.'

'I meant to come over in the morning, but I had one meeting after another. How was your day?'

'Good,' she said. 'I think I'm going to like working here.'

'Did Venkat manage to spend any time with you?'

'A lot,' she said drily.

Darius laughed. 'He believes in throwing people in at the deep end,' he said. 'But he's a great guy to work with. If you're done for the day d'you want to catch up over coffee? There's a decent café nearby.'

Mallika hesitated. She really wanted to confront Darius about him leaving, but her upbringing made her shy away from any kind of direct conflict.

Some of her indecision must have shown in her face, because he was beginning to look puzzled.

'Or some other day if you need to leave,' he said easily.

Mallika made up her mind.

'I need to get home, but I have time for a coffee from the machine down the hall,' she said.

Compromise—that was one thing she'd learnt early in life. And also that attacking issues head-on sometimes made them worse. She got to her feet and Darius followed her down the hall.

'On second thoughts, I'll have a soft drink,' she said, taking a can from the fridge next to the coffee dispenser. 'You can have that coffee if you want,' she said, gesturing at the mug Darius had just filled for her.

She picked up a second mug and half filled it with warm water from the machine before putting her unopened can into it.

'It's too cold,' she explained as Darius raised his eyebrows. 'I'll leave it in the mug for a bit and then it'll be just right and I'll drink it.'

Darius's lips curved into a smile as he followed Mallika back to her room. She was wearing black trousers, a no-nonsense blue shirt, and extremely sensible shoes. The whole outfit looked as if it had been chosen to downplay her looks, but the most boring clothes in the world couldn't conceal the narrowness of her waist and the athletic grace of her walk. Quite contrary to the intended effect, the clothes made her *more* appealing—at least to him.

'Is Venkat involved in the day-to-day running of the fund?' she asked, perching herself on the edge of her desk and swinging her legs idly.

'Not really…' he said cautiously, and she gave him a quizzical look, 'Okay, he's *very* involved in it—but his area of expertise is sales. You won't be reporting to him, if that's your worry—all the directors report straight to the board.'

'Hmm…no, that isn't what was bothering me.'

She smiled at him, and Darius felt his heartbeat quicken in response.

'But tell me—is it true that he's interfered in some of the investment decisions the team have made in the past?'

It was very likely to be true. Darius had heard rumblings from his team, but he hadn't paid much attention up till now. Mallika's pointing it out after being exactly one day in the job, however, hit him on the raw.

'He's talked to them about a few deals,' he said. 'I wouldn't go so far as to call it interference.'

'Maybe it wasn't brought to your attention, then,' she said, clearly unfazed by the sudden chilliness in his tone. 'But he's made some bad calls, and the fund's asset value has dropped. It'll take me a while to undo the damage.'

It was her air of knowing exactly what to do that got to him.

'I'd suggest you take a few days to understand the business properly first,' he said firmly, though he was feeling uncharacteristically defensive. 'Before you jump in with both feet and start undoing things.'

Mallika frowned. 'I thought the whole point of my being here was that I already know the business,' she said. 'I researched the fund before I even started interviewing with you guys, and it's obvious that you have problems. Logically, it makes no sense to wait to fix them.'

'There's a lot of stuff you wouldn't know from the outside,' Darius insisted. 'Venkat might have his...quirks, but not all the decisions he's made have been bad.'

She shrugged. 'Statistically speaking, even if you made decisions by rolling dice you would end up making some decent ones. But from what I can make out Venkat is superstitious, and his judgement is coloured.'

It had taken Darius months to realise that Venkat's superstitious side sometimes overruled his normally sharp business brain. Mallika had taken exactly one day to figure it out. She was extraordinarily perceptive and he felt slightly wrong-footed. *Again.*

What was this woman doing to him?

Mallika was leaning forward a little. 'Look, you hired me to run this fund,' she said. 'Not because you liked my face. So let me get on with my work. If I mess up you can play the hero and come in and rescue me.'

For a second Darius was tempted to tell her exactly how much he liked her face, but hard as it was he bit back the words. Being her colleague meant that he had to keep a certain professional distance. Speaking of which… Darius realised just how close he was to Mallika, and rolled his chair a few paces back. Unfortunately as soon as he started to speak again Mallika scooted her shapely butt closer to him once more, robbing him of his train of thought.

'You're right about Venkat,' he said, trying to sound as detached as possible. 'The whole superstition thing….' He hesitated a little while trying to find the right words. 'It's a little…'

'Kooky?' she supplied, putting her head to one side. 'Eccentric? Odd?'

'Unconventional,' he said. 'But it's not uncommon.'

'And it's unimportant too, I assume?' she said before she could stop herself. 'As far as you're concerned anyway. Because you're not planning to be around when the problems kick in.'

If she'd expected him to look guilty she was disappointed, because he threw his head back and laughed. 'I mightn't be around, but the fund's performance is still pretty damn important to me. I have a fair bit of my own money invested in it, and I don't fancy seeing it go down the tube.'

'I suppose I should be flattered,' she said drily. 'Here I was, thinking you'd given me the fund to run because you didn't care what happened to it.'

'And now you know I've put my life's savings in your hands,' he said. 'Who told you I was moving out? Venkat?'

'Yes,' she said.

'It's not supposed to be public knowledge yet,' he said. 'The board has asked me to stay on for a few months, and they felt it best that the rest of the firm be told I'm leaving only when it's a lot closer to my last day here.'

'Funny…Venkat assumed you'd already told me,' she said. 'Perhaps he thought it was only fair—given that you recruited me and everything.'

Darius leaned a little closer, his brow creasing. 'Are you annoyed that I didn't tell you?' he demanded, putting a hand under her chin to tip her face upwards. 'Even after what I just said?'

Mallika jerked her head away, trying to ignore the little thrill that went through her at his touch.

'Not annoyed…just a little…concerned,' she said, hoping her words would hide how much she longed to work alongside this charismatic man. 'There might be other things you omitted to mention. I pretty much took everything you said at face value.'

'Now, wait a minute,' he said incredulously. 'Are you suggesting I *lied* to you about the job? What makes you think that?'

'You weren't open at all,' she said. 'All this while you've let me think that you'd be around—that you were simply taking on something within the firm. If I'd known you were leaving…'

'You wouldn't have joined?' He looked quite genuinely puzzled. 'Why not? You seem like you have a handle on things already. My being here or not doesn't make a difference, surely?'

Darius was struggling to keep a smug smile off his face—he wasn't the only one who felt what was between them then.

Oh, but it does, Mallika almost said. The thought of working at Nidas without Darius was unsettling in a not very nice way, and she had to scramble to think of a logical explanation for her anxiety.

'I'm just wondering why you're leaving,' she said. 'I something's going wrong with the company… And I did discuss my working hours with you…'

His brow cleared immediately. 'Oh, the flexi-time thing?' he said. 'Don't worry about that at all—I've cleared it with the board. And give Venkat some time— he's a great guy to work with once you get past his superstitious streak.'

He was probably right—he'd worked with Venkat for years, after all, and she'd only met the man today. And she hadn't known Darius for very long either—there was absolutely no reason for the sinking feeling in the pit of her stomach when she thought about him leaving Nidas.

'Hmm….' she said. 'I think I'll get along well with Venkat—I'll have to. I'll need a lot of help from him for the first few months.'

'Will you?' he asked, feeling oddly jealous.

If Mallika needed help *he'd* have liked to be the one to provide it. For a few seconds before his rational side had kicked in he'd actually thought that she was upset because she'd miss him. Now he was left with an absurd feeling of being sidelined—just another stepping stone in Mallika's life.

Their timing was completely off, he thought ruefully. If he'd met her either a couple of years earlier or later he'd have tried to get to know her better—perhaps even acted on the growing attraction between the two of them. Right now it was completely out of the question. By the time they were no longer colleagues he'd be long gone.

'You still haven't told me why you're leaving,' Mallika said, and he blinked.

'Personal reasons,' he said, standing up to leave. 'Don't worry—the company's not about to go under.'

Mallika laughed at that. She had a particularly appealing laugh, Darius thought. It was as happy and uncomplicated as a child's, but it had a woman's maturity as well, and a sexy little undertone that was irresistible.

'That's reassuring,' she said, slipping off the desk to land on her feet right next to him.

Darius looked into her eyes and there was an instant of absolute connection that made his earlier thoughts irrelevant. A small part of his brain recognised how clichéd the moment was, and he was even amused. The rest of him was completely overwhelmed, and he kept on looking at her stupidly until she blinked and looked away.

'Goodness, look at the time!' she said, her voice slightly more high-pitched than normal. 'I really need to get going.'

'You haven't touched your drink,' he said, and she blinked at the can as if it had just materialised on her desk. 'I'll...um...carry it with me,' she said. 'What about your coffee?'

'I hate that stuff from the machine,' he said. 'Next time we'll go to a proper café.'

The way he said it made it sound like a promise he couldn't wait to keep.

'See you around, Darius,' she managed to squeak, before making a hasty exit.

The next time he saw her was a few days later, with over fifty other people in the same room. Venkat had called for an investor conference, and Mallika was the main presenter.

Darius came in late, slipping into the back of the room. He very rarely attended investor events, but Venkat had been unusually insistent, and he hadn't been able to resist the thought of seeing Mallika in top professional mode.

She was an impressive speaker—economical with words, but leaving her listeners with no doubt of her grasp over the subject. Slim and graceful in a raw silk printed sari, she exuded an aura of confidence and authority that was strangely attractive. Some people would probably think that it detracted from her femininity but, standing at the back of the room, Darius had to work hard to maintain a professional veneer.

She was quite something.

'She's brilliant, isn't she?' Venkat said, materialising next to Darius.

Mallika was answering a question raised by a grizzled investor old enough to be her father—and by the way the rest of the audience was nodding they were as impressed as Venkat was.

'It's been a while since we've held an event of this sort—it's bloody expensive, paying for the dinner and the booze, but it's worth it if we get the monies to come in. And people *are* interested—the market's looking up. We'll get a couple of hundred crores of investment after this event.'

'So does that mean you guys are doing perfectly well without me?' Darius asked, giving Venkat an amused look.

'We are,' Venkat said. 'Mallika's probably the best person you could have hired to replace you—in spite of all that flexible working rubbish. But, man, this place isn't going to be the same without you.'

The event wound to a close, and Mallika stepped off the dais to mingle with the guests. Venkat had been called back for the vote of thanks, and Darius stood alone at the back of the room, watching Mallika as she moved from one group of middle-aged men to the next, her smile firmly in place.

There were only a handful of women in the audience, and Darius noted that she spent longer with them, explaining something at length to one group and patiently allowing a much older woman to peer at the necklace of semi-precious stones she was wearing.

It was a while before the audience dispersed, most of them heading towards the buffet dinner.

Mallika's shoulders sagged a tiny bit, and the smile left her face as she walked towards the exit. It was as if she'd turnedt off a switch, changing from a confident, sparkling professional to a young woman who was just a little tired with life.

Darius waved to her, and she came across to him.

'I didn't see you come in,' she said. 'Did you just get here?'

'A while ago,' he said. 'I'm impressed, Mallika. You had everyone eating out of your hands.'

She shrugged. 'I've done this kind of event many times before,' she said. 'They're exhausting, but it's part of my job.'

'What do you find exhausting?' Darius asked.

'Talking to people,' she said. 'It's a strain. Everyone asks the same questions, and by the end of it I get so sick I could scream. Don't tell Venkat,' she added, looking up with a quick smile that lit up her face. 'He's planning a whole series of these events.'

'I was about to tell you that,' Darius said, a smile tugging at his lips. 'He's thrilled with the way you handled this one.' She made a little grimace, and a spurt of chivalry made Darius ask, 'Should I talk to him? He can handle the events himself—or one of the other fund managers could speak in your place.'

'The other fund managers aren't lucky for Venkat,' she said drily. 'I doubt he'll agree. Anyway, it's part of why you hired me, right?'

Darius nodded. It had been unprofessional of him to suggest he intervene, and he couldn't help admire Mallika's determination to do every part of her job well. Even when she obviously hated what she was doing.

It was intriguing, the way her ultra-professional mask slipped at times to betray her vulnerability. He had a feeling she didn't let it happen often, and all his protective instincts surged to the forefront whenever it did.

'Aren't you having dinner?' Venkat asked, popping up next to them. 'Or a drink? Mallika?'

She shook her head. 'I need to leave,' she said. 'My driver's taken the day off, so I've called a cab. The cabbie's been waiting for half an hour already.'

'Wouldn't it have been simpler to drive yourself?'

'I don't drive,' she said. 'I've tried learning a few times, but it's been an unmitigated disaster.'

'And you don't drink either! What a waste,' Venkat said sorrowfully. In his opinion, the best part of an event of this sort was the company-sponsored alcohol. 'Darius?'

Darius shook his head. 'I need to leave as well,' he

said. 'Got some people coming over. And I'm driving, so I can't have a drink either.'

Venkat looked ridiculously disappointed, and Darius laughed, clapping him on the shoulder.

'I'll take you out for a drink this Friday,' he promised. 'Come on, Mallika—I'll walk you to the lobby.'

Their event had been held in a rather exclusive mid-town hotel, and there were several other corporate events in full swing there. The banquet hall next to theirs was hosting an annual party, and the waiting area outside the banquet hall was dotted with entertainers. Jugglers in clown costumes, living statues, and even a magician or two.

Mallika paused next to a gigantic plastic sphere with a girl playing the violin inside it, and stared at it critically.

'What's the idea?' she asked. 'Why's the girl in the bubble?'

Darius shrugged. 'It's supposed to add a touch of the exotic,' he said. 'In the last party I went to of this sort they'd flown in a belly dancer from Turkey to dance for about ten minutes.'

'Ugh, what an awful job,' Mallika said, wondering which was worse—the few men who were openly leering at the blonde violinist in her low-cut green Tinker Bell dress, or the people who were walking past without even acknowledging her as a human being. 'I'm suddenly feeling a lot better about my own work.'

'No plastic bubbles?' Darius said solemnly as they went down the stairs that led to the hotel lobby. 'That *is* a significant upside, I agree. And wonderful colleagues to work with, perhaps?'

She giggled. 'Like Venkat?'

'Like *me*, I was going to say.' Darius held the door

open for her as they went out into the night air. 'But clearly I've not done enough to impress you yet.'

Mallika looked up at him. In the warm light pouring out from the lobby he looked incredible. His hair was slightly mussed, and a few strands fell over his forehead in sexy disarray. He'd come from work, but he'd taken off his tie and undone the top button of his shirt, and it was difficult to take her eyes off the triangle of exposed skin. And when she did it was only to lose herself in *his* eyes—dark and amused, with a hint of something that was disturbingly exciting.

'Consider me impressed,' she said lightly, and turned away to dig for her phone in her bag, ignoring the sudden movement he made towards her.

'What d'you mean, you've *left*?' she demanded a few minutes later, having finally got through to the cabbie.

She listened to what sounded like an incredibly complicated explanation, and sighed.

'He got another fare and went off,' she said. 'I'll have to ask the hotel to get me a cab.'

'Or I could drop you home?' Darius suggested.

'Isn't it out of your way?'

'Not terribly,' Darius lied. 'We'll take the sea link.' Dropping Mallika home would add forty-five minutes to his drive, but it was worth it.

'If you're sure, then,' Mallika said, heaving a sigh of relief.

It wouldn't be difficult getting another cab back, but the thought of the lonely drive home was singularly depressing. And, whether she admitted it to herself or not, the prospect of spending more time with Darius held a lot of appeal.

Darius handed his valet parking token to an attendant

and put a hand under Mallika's elbow as he steered her to one side. By Mumbai standards it was unusually chilly, and there was a strong breeze blowing. He felt Mallika shiver a little, and gave her a concerned look.

'Do you have a wrap or something?' he asked, and she shook her head, drawing the *pallu* of her sari around her shoulders.

'No, I didn't think it would be cold,' she said.

'And I've left my jacket in my car,' Darius said. 'All my life I've wanted to be chivalrous like in movies—put my jacket around a shivering girl's shoulders—and when I get the perfect opportunity...'

'You find you've forgotten the jacket?' she said, laughing up at him. 'Don't worry about it—I'm not likely to die of frostbite.'

'You could catch a cold, though,' he said, sounding quite serious. 'I'll take you back inside till the car comes up.'

Or you could put your arm around me, Mallika almost said. That would be another favourite Hollywood moment, copied faithfully by Bollywood in multiple movies. Even suggesting it was out of the question, of course, but oh, how she wished she could!

Before she could turn around, a slim woman with waist-length hair came up to them and tapped Darius lightly on the shoulder. A man followed her, a long-suffering look on his face.

'It's Tubby Mistry, isn't it?' she asked, after hesitating a little.

Darius looked around, his face breaking into a smile. 'Nivi! How are you doing?'

'It *is* you!' the woman said, giving a little squeal of delight before throwing herself into his arms.

The man, presumably her husband, gave Mallika a resigned look. Mallika smiled at him, though inwardly she was feeling absurdly jealous of the woman. It was particularly ironic, her turning up and flinging herself into Darius's arms just when Mallika had been wishing she could do exactly that.

'My goodness, I almost didn't recognise you,' Nivi said, stepping back after giving Darius several exuberant hugs and leaving a lipstick mark on his cheek. 'I spotted you when you were walking out of the hotel. You looked so familiar, but I just couldn't place you.'

'She thought you were a TV celeb,' her husband interjected, earning himself a reproachful look.

'You can't blame me for that—he's turned out so utterly gorgeous!' she said. 'You should have seen him in school! He was overweight and gawky and he wore a perfectly hideous pair of glasses. No girl would have turned to look at him twice.'

Her husband cleared his throat, jerking his head towards Mallika.

'Oh, I'm so sorry,' Nivi said, looking genuinely contrite. 'You don't mind, do you? I'm Nivedita. I knew Darius in school, and we've not met in years. I moved back to Kolkata, and I've lived there ever since. We only got here today, and he's the first person I've met from my old life.'

'You must send me some of his school pictures,' Mallika said promptly, and Darius groaned.

'Nivi, if you do anything of that sort I'll have to break that solemn blood oath you made me swear in school.'

'Blackmailer!' she said, giving him another affectionate hug. 'Don't you dare, Darius. Remember all the help I gave you for your Hindi exams?'

' 'Yes, well, I passed the exams, but I still can't speak a sentence without making mistakes,' he said, and Nivedita laughed.

'You'll learn the language some day,' she said. 'Okay, I'm off now—I can see the two of you are dying to be alone. I'll get in touch with you soon, Tubby.'

'It's our *karma,*' Darius said sadly once Nivedita and her long-suffering husband were out of earshot. 'Faces from the past popping up wherever we go.'

'It's happened exactly once for me—and that time it was a face from the present,' Mallika retorted. 'And Vaishali didn't start drawing up a list of my most embarrassing moments for the whole world to hear.'

'What can I say? Your past isn't as chequered as mine,' Darius said as he took his car keys from the valet parking attendant. 'Come on, let's go.'

'You said Nivedita swore you to a blood oath when you were in school,' Mallika said curiously after she got into the car. 'What was that about?'

'I caught her kissing our house captain,' Darius said as he manoeuvred the car out of a particularly complicated set of barricades at the hotel exit.

'Would that matter now? I'm sure her husband wouldn't be particularly shocked.'

'The house captain was a girl,' Darius said, grinning as Mallika's jaw dropped. 'Nivi was going through an experimental phase.'

'I suppose she finally decided that she preferred men,' Mallika said. 'Bit of a loudmouth isn't she? Were you really that hideous, or was she exaggerating?'

Darius sighed. 'I was a blimp,' he said. 'I weighed almost a hundred kilos and I wore glasses. My mother loved baking, and I loved eating. Luckily I managed to get into my school football team, and the coach made me run twenty rounds of the field every day before the others even turned up for practice. I was down to skin and bone in three months.'

'That explains a lot,' she said, and as he gave her a quizzical look went on, 'You're not vain about your looks. Most good-looking men act like they're doing you a favour by allowing you to breathe the same air as them.'

Darius, who hardly ever thought about his looks at all, felt absurdly flattered. He knew he was a lot more attractive now than he'd been in his schooldays, but he hadn't realised that Mallika liked the way he looked.

'So what happened to the spectacles?' Mallika asked. 'Contact lenses?'

'Laser correction,' Darius said. 'D'you realise you sound like you're interviewing me for a reality show?'

'Serves you right for having become so good-looking,' Mallika said.

They were heading onto the highway that connected North Mumbai to South, and she groaned as she caught sight of a sea of cars.

'We'll be here for ever!' she said. 'There's a new fly-over being built, and three of the six lanes are blocked off.'

'If you'd told me just a little earlier I'd have taken a different route,' Darius murmured, edging the car into the least sluggish lane.

'They're all as bad,' she said, sighing. 'Anyway, at least we have each other for company.' There was a short pause after which Mallika said, 'Darius, can I ask you something?'

'Yes,' he said, though his eyes were still on the road. 'Ask away.'

'Where are you going to be working after you leave Nidas?'

She'd expected him to say that he'd got a better offer from a competitor, or perhaps that he was working on a new start-up. What he actually said came as a complete surprise.

'Nowhere,' he said, as casually as if it was the most obvious answer.

Mallika waited a bit, but when he didn't qualify his answer she said tentatively, 'What are you planning to do, then?'

He turned to give her a quick smile.

'Travel,' he said. 'And some volunteer work—but only after a year or so. For the first year I'm planning on Europe and Africa, perhaps a few months in China and Russia. I've made enough money to last me for several years—if it runs out I'm sure I'll find some way of making some more.'

'You're serious?' Mallika asked. 'I mean, I know people do that kind of thing in the West, but I've never heard of anyone in India quitting their job just to...*travel*.'

The way she said 'travel' was impossibly cute, as if it was a strange, slightly dangerous word that she was trying out for the first time—Darius found his lips curving automatically into a smile.

'I'm serious,' he said. 'Not planning to work for the next five years at least. After that... Well, I'll figure it out when I need to.'

Mallika sat silent for a few minutes, trying to digest what she'd just heard. Darius had struck her as a responsible, steady sort of a man—the last kind of man she'd have expected to leave his job and go wandering around the world on a whim. Showed how bad she was at reading people, she thought. Her own father had been careless to the point of being irresponsible, but this was the first time she'd met someone who was consciously and collectedly plunging into uncertainty.

'You don't approve?' Darius asked wryly as the silence stretched on.

She shook her head in confusion, 'It's not that,' she said. 'It's not my place to approve or disapprove—it just seems like such a drastic thing to do. I guess I don't understand why. I mean, you can travel on holidays, can't you? And what about your family?'

'My family understands,' he said. 'They're as crazy as I am, and they won't let a small thing like my being on a different continent affect the way they feel about me. And travelling on holiday isn't the same thing as being completely free, exploring and having adventures. Setting up Nidas was great, and I've loved that part of my life. But now that it's a success it's slowly becoming like any other large company. I don't find it as fulfilling as I did in the days when we were struggling to make a mark. I wasn't born to be a corporate suit.'

'Unlike me,' Mallika said with a little smile. 'I love the structure and safety of working for a large company.'

Her mother had set up a successful business of her own, but she'd hated the uncertainty and the ups and downs, and she'd taught Mallika to hate them as well.

Before he could reply her phone rang, and she frowned as she took the call.

'Hi, Aryan... Yes, I'm on my way back... No, I'm not coming that way. I'm taking the sea link... No, I can't, Aryan. I've taken a lift from someone, it's completely out of our way, and I'm exhausted.' There was a brief pause, and then she said wearily, 'Aryan, can't this wait till Saturday?'

Evidently it couldn't.

'Look, I'll do my best, but I'm not promising anything. Message me the specs.'

She stared out of the window unseeingly, and Darius hesitated a little before asking quietly, 'Everything okay?'

Mallika turned towards him. 'Yes,' she said with a sigh. 'My brother wants a new memory card for his camera. Actually for my camera—he's sort of taken it over, because I don't have time for photography any longer. I just got a little upset with him because he wants me to stop and buy it for him right now.'

'We can stop if you like,' Darius said, wondering why Aryan didn't go and buy the memory card himself. Maybe he was a little spoilt, and used to his sister running errands for him.

'No, it's fine,' Mallika said. 'I'll try calling a few stores and if they have it I'll get off at the nearest point and take a cab.'

'Assuming they're still open by the time we get to South Mumbai,' Darius said, indicating the traffic outside. 'It's already past nine.'

'So it is,' Mallika said.

Her phone pinged and she glanced down, laughing in spite of herself.

'He's figured out there's a shop that sells memory cards and is open till ten-thirty,' she said. 'And he's told the guy who owns it to wait until I get there.'

'Is it on the way?' Darius asked.

Mallika shook her head. 'No, it's in Worli. You can

drop me where the sea link ends and then you can go home. It'll save you some time. I can grab a cab.'

'I'll come with you,' Darius said, feeling unreasonably irritated with Mallika as well as with Aryan. 'I'm not sure how safe it is, you traipsing around on your own in the middle of the night.'

'It's perfectly safe,' Mallika said crisply. 'But if you're sure it's not inconvenient...' Here, her lips curved into a disarmingly lovely smile. 'I'd love it if you came along.'

'It's not inconvenient,' Darius said, and it took all his self-control not to lean across and kiss her.

Clearly Mallika didn't believe in the fine art of dissembling—if she wanted him around she came right out and said so, instead of pretending that she'd just feel safer if he came with her. It was an unusual and refreshing trait in a woman, and Darius felt himself fall just a little bit in love with her as he smiled back.

'Aryan isn't as spoilt as he seems,' Mallika said suddenly. 'He's got a bit of an issue with stepping out of the house.'

'His health?' Darius asked.

She shook her head. 'No, it's more of a mental thing. He was pretty badly affected when our parents died, but he didn't show it for a while. And then he started going out less and less, and now he doesn't step out at all. And he doesn't like people coming over, though he's usually okay talking on the phone. That time we went out for lunch and I had to leave—my aunt had come over to look after him and he refused to answer the doorbell. She thought something had happened to him, and she was so upset when she found out that he was perfectly okay—just not in the mood to open the door.'

She ground to a halt, wondering why she'd said so

much. Aryan and his peculiarities weren't a good subject for casual conversation.

'So that's why you need a flexible working arrange-
ment,' Darius said slowly, a lot of things he'd found odd
about Mallika clicking into place. 'I'm so sorry. I didn't
realise that your parents....'

'They died in an accident,' she said hurriedly. 'It was
more than two years ago. I don't talk about it much, but
it gets more awkward the later I leave it.'

'I get that,' he said, and he looked as if he truly did.

Most people she told either looked awkward or felt
terribly sorry for her and gushed over her—both reactions made holding on to her temper tough. Darius
looked sympathetic, but not pitying.

'Car accident?' he asked, and she shook her head.

'Gas cylinder explosion,' she said, and he winced.

'That sucks,' he said. 'I'm sorry. Come on, the traffic's finally moving—let's go and get that memory card.'

He kept the conversation light until they'd picked up
the memory card—the shop was in an unsavoury little
lane, and his lips tightened a little as he thought of Mallika going there alone. He didn't say anything, however,
answering her questions on his travel plans instead, and
listening to her stories of a holiday in Switzerland that
she'd taken with her mother.

It was the first time that Mallika had really opened up
and talked, and Darius found his respect for her growing as he listened. She had obviously been very close to
her mother, but she was handling her loss with dignity
and restraint. Darius had been through his share of family problems, and he could catch the undertone of strain
in her voice when she mentioned Aryan. But she didn't
complain, and Aryan's name only came up in the context

of a hilarious scrap she'd got into with an online clothing store when they'd delivered a set of women's underwear instead of the shirt Aryan had ordered.

Darius still got the impression that ever since their parents died she'd made Aryan the sole focus of her life, and that she felt deeply responsible for him.

They were almost at her flat when he asked, 'Have you tried taking Aryan to a doctor?'

'Several times,' Mallika said. 'Nothing's worked. You see, he needs to be interested in getting better. Right now, he doesn't want that. He seems happy as he is.'

Darius wished he could ask her if *she* was happy, but it was too personal a question, so he contented himself with giving her a light hug before she got out of the car. Her hair smelt of orange blossom and bergamot, and her slim arms were warm and strong around his neck as she hugged him back.

'Thanks,' she said as she straightened up. 'For dropping me home, and for listening to me chatter about things.'

She turned and went into her apartment block quickly, and she heard him start the car and drive away as she got into the lift. The lift man was off duty and the lift was empty—Mallika got in and pulled the old-fashioned door shut behind her before sagging onto the lift man's chair.

It had been a long while since she'd last talked about her family, and the conversation with Darius had brought the memories flooding back. For perhaps the hundredth time she wished she'd gone with her family to Alibagh that weekend.

It had been one of those totally pointless accidents— the kind that could have been avoided easily if only someone had been around at the right time. The cylinder of cooking gas had probably been leaking slowly for a while, but her mother hadn't smelt it because she'd had a cold. She'd picked up the lighter and clicked it on to light the gas stove, the way she did every evening—only this time there'd been a swooshing sound as the petroleum gas pervading the air had caught fire.

Her mother had screamed once, and the scream had brought her father rushing to the kitchen.

They hadn't stood a chance.

The wall of flame had hit the leaking cylinder, and the spare one next to it, and in the next second both cylinders had exploded, turning the kitchen into a blazing inferno. Aryan had been outside in the garden, but he hadn't been able to get anywhere near his parents. And Alibagh was a small, sleepy seaside town—it had been almost twenty minutes before a fire engine reached the house.

It had been in time to save the rest of the house, but far too late to save Mallika's parents. The firemen had told her later that both of them must have died within a few minutes of the explosion, and her only consolation was that at least it must have been quick.

She'd been in shock, but she'd managed to hold herself together long enough to let her relatives know, organise the funeral, and get her brother back to Mumbai. Then, when everything was done, and she'd been about ready to fall apart in private, she'd realised that something was seriously wrong with her brother.

CHAPTER FOUR

MALLIKA KNEW SHE was going to be at work late the next day. A neighbour had complained about Aryan's habit of taking photographs from the windows using a telescopic lens—apparently she thought he was spying on her. It had taken some time to soothe her ruffled feathers, and now Mallika had spent almost an hour trying to explain to Aryan that he couldn't go around peering into other people's houses.

'I was trying to take a picture of a crow on her windowsill,' he said. 'I mean, look at her—d'you think it's likely I'd want a picture of *her* taking up disk space?'

'She doesn't know that,' Mallika said, as patiently as she could. 'And that was *my* camera you were using without asking me. Aryan, look…things are tough enough without you trying to make them tougher. Be a little more considerate, will you? Please?'

He didn't reply, and she almost gave up. Another woman in her place might have lost her temper, or created a scene, but Mallika had had years of training from her mother. However upset she'd been, she'd always concealed her true feelings from the men of the family and soldiered on. For years she'd watched her mother deal with her grandfather and father, and with Aryan as he grew up—the other two men were gone now, and so was her mother, but Mallika found it difficult to shake old habits.

'I'll see you this evening, then,' she said. 'Make sure you eat your lunch, okay?'

He mumbled something that she couldn't catch.

'I didn't get that,' she said.

'I'm sorry,' he whispered, without looking up. 'I didn't mean to upset you.'

Mallika felt her heart twist painfully within her. Aryan was demanding, and sometimes troublesome, but he was very different from her father—and he was the only part of her family left to her.

She went across to him and patted his shoulder awkwardly. 'It's all right,' she said. 'Just be a little careful, *baba*. We can't afford to antagonise the neighbours.'

'I'll be careful,' he said, and looked up, his eyes pleading. 'Do you *have* to go to work?' he asked. 'Can't you work from home today?'

Mallika hesitated. She *could* work from home, but the last time she'd spoken to Aryan's doctor he'd told her that she should try and gently wean him from his excessive dependence on her. She hated leaving him when he'd asked her to stay—it filled her with guilt and worry. But she knew she had to do what was best for Aryan, to try and help him. He was her responsibility.

'I'll come back early,' she promised. 'Why don't you go downstairs and sit in the garden for a bit? Then when I come back we can try going for a drive. Wouldn't that be fun?'

Aryan's face clouded over and he shook his head. 'No,' he said.

Mallika sighed. She'd been trying for months to get Aryan to step out of the flat with absolutely zero success. 'Why, Aryan?' she asked. 'I know you're finding it tough without Mum and Dad, but you need to try and get back to normal. I'll be with you—we don't even need to go anywhere far…'

His grip on her hand tightened painfully. 'I just… can't.' he said, and she had to be content with that.

She couldn't push him any further. If he didn't want to get better she couldn't make him. Something had broken in Aryan when their parents died, and all her love didn't seem enough to set it right.

Her phone was ringing as she let herself into her room at work an hour later.

'Nidas Investments, Mallika speaking,' she said automatically as she picked up the phone without looking at the caller ID.

'Very businesslike,' a familiar voice said approvingly, and her mood was immediately lifted by several notches.

The scene with Aryan had left her feeling drained and helpless, but just the sound of Darius's voice made the world seem like a better place.

'I've called to ask you for some help,' he said. 'I'm looking for a flat to rent, and I'm kind of desperate now. Since you know the real estate business inside out…'

'Don't you have a flat of your own already?'

'It's a long story,' he said. 'I have a flat in the same building as my parents. My sister's moving back to India, and I offered it to her when I thought I'd be leaving Nidas this month. But now that the board's asked me to stay on for another three months I need a place to stay. Only it's difficult to get somewhere for three months—I'm okay with paying rent for six, but not too many people offer leases that short. I really liked a condo in Parel, but it got snapped up by the time I got around to making an offer.'

'That's a pity,' Mallika said, wondering what kind of flat Darius would like. You could tell a lot about a person from the type of home they chose, and she thought she could picture the kind he'd go for. Big, airy and luxurious, but in an understated way. 'Which building?'

He told her, and added, 'It was a great flat—really large living room, with a massive balcony and two bedrooms. But there are only a few flats in the building with that plan. The rest have normal-sized living rooms.'

'Yes, it's only the flats next to the fire refuge areas that have that layout,' Mallika said, chewing her lip thoughtfully. 'I know the building pretty well.'

She was silent for a few seconds, and Darius could hear her slow, careful breathing over the phone line.

'If you're really keen on a flat like that I might be able to get you one for three months,' she said. 'Reasonable rent, and you won't have to pay brokerage. But you'd need to keep the flat in good condition, be careful not to upset the neighbours and all that.'

'I'm keen,' he said, smiling slightly at her tone. 'And I'm housetrained.'

'Hmm...' she said, as if she was only partially convinced. 'Meet me in the parking lot at lunchtime—say at around one—and I can take you to see the flat. It won't take more than half an hour.'

'You mean today?'

'You were the one who said you were keen!'

'So I did.' Darius got to his feet. 'We'll take my car. See you downstairs at one.'

The building was only a couple of kilometres away, and Darius crossed his fingers as they drove through the gate.

He'd been trying to make the best of it, but living with his parents again after a gap of fourteen years was far more stressful than he'd anticipated. So far he'd found only that one place to rent that he'd liked, and he'd been seriously considering choosing one at random from the row of sub-par flats and service apartments his agent had lined up for him.

Mallika's suggestion was a godsend—even if the flat wasn't precisely the same layout as the one he'd initially chosen he was inclined to take it.

He glanced across at her. She was more casually dressed than usual—perhaps because she had no meetings to attend. A black top in some silky material clung lovingly to her curves, and he could see a tantalising hint of cleavage. Her trousers were well cut, and her shoes as sensible as always—the only dash of colour in her outfit was provided by a turquoise blue stole that matched her leather tote.

'You always carry a funky handbag,' he said suddenly as a security guard waved the car to a stop just inside the gate. 'But you wear sensible-looking shoes. Not seen too many girls do that—it's usually neither or both.'

She gave him a quick smile. 'I can't wear heels,' she said. 'Always trip and fall over. But I love bags, and I buy a new one almost every month. I'm surprised you noticed.'

She wasn't just surprised, she was also flattered he'd paid that much attention. Most men didn't notice anything about women's fashions beyond necklines and hemlines.

'I've grown up with a shopaholic sister,' he said, laughing. 'And every girlfriend I've ever had has been crazy about shoes and bags.'

Mallika wrinkled her nose a little at the thought of his girlfriends—she was sure he'd had several, and she found herself thinking negative thoughts about all of them.

The security guard came up to the car and Mallika had to get out and talk to him. Darius tapped the wheel idly as he looked out across the sprawling private garden that was one of the most attractive features of the building.

A tall man came out of the main entrance, and Mallika smiled at him, driving all thoughts of property prices out of Darius's head. The man put an arm around Mallika and gave her a hug that was halfway between friendly and proprietorial, and Darius felt an unfamiliar surge of jealousy as Mallika hugged him back. He knew that Mallika wasn't in a relationship, and it hadn't occurred to him that she might have close male friends. The thought was surprisingly unsettling.

'I have the keys,' Mallika said, sliding back into the passenger seat. 'There's parking for visitors at the back of the building. Take a left after the ramp... Left, Darius—*this* is your left.'

She tugged at his arm as he narrowly missed driving into a flowerbed and Darius grinned as he swung the wheel to the left. 'Sorry, I'm a bit directionally challenged,' he said. 'Especially when bossy women bark into my ear.'

'I'm not bossy!' Mallika protested. She'd let her hand linger on his arm a bit longer than strictly necessary, and now she squeezed it hard. 'Park by the wall. No, not behind the truck—there's more space behind that little red car.'

'Not bossy in the least,' Darius murmured, and she made a face as she got out of the car.

'I'm bossy only when the situation demands it,' she said, linking her arm through his. 'Come on, let's go see the flat.'

'Who was the man you were talking to outside?' he asked as they walked towards the building. 'The guy who gave you the keys? You seemed to know him pretty well.'

He sounded faintly jealous, and Mallika felt her mood improve even further.

'He's an old friend,' she said. 'We were at college together, and he worked with my mother for a while. He and his wife bought a place here last year, and they've been keeping an eye on the flat I'm taking you to.'

Darius nodded. It was ridiculous—it shouldn't matter to him in the least—but he felt a lot better now that he knew the man was married.

The lift man saluted when they got into the lift, and Mallika gave him a quick smile.

'Twentieth floor,' she said, and the man nodded.

'*Sahib* is going to stay here?' he asked.

'*Sahib* is going to figure out first if he likes it or not,' Mallika said. 'What do you think, Shinde? Will he like it?'

'*Sahib* will like it definitely,' Shinde said.

His expression suggested that *sahib* would have to be a blithering idiot not to like it, and Darius suppressed a smile. Mallika had an automatic air of command that Shinde was clearly not immune to—if she'd said that she was taking Darius up to the twentieth floor to persuade him to jump off it she would probably still have had Shinde's wholehearted support.

'It's a beautiful flat, madam,' Shinde added, giving

Darius a disapproving look as the lift doors opened at the twentieth floor.

Shinde was right—the flat *was* beautiful. The layout, of course, was excellent, with a living room that was huge by Mumbai standards, two respectable-sized bedrooms and a compact but very well-designed kitchen. Unlike the stark, unfurnished flat Darius had seen the last time he'd come to the building, this one was fully furnished—right down to elegant white leather sofas and sheer silver curtains with a blue thread running through them.

The colour scheme was predominantly blue and white, but lampshades and rugs made little splashes of vibrant colour. There were a couple of framed vintage Bollywood posters on one wall, while another had a collection of masks from across the country. The overall effect was one of laid-back luxury, and Darius could imagine a high-end interior designer working very hard to produce it.

'You can get rid of the posters and the masks, if you like,' Mallika said as she walked across the room to open the large French windows leading onto the balcony. 'And if you have furniture of your own we can get this put in storage.'

Darius followed her out onto the balcony. The flat overlooked a racecourse and the view was amazing. It was an unusually clear day, and the sea shimmered in the distance, the steel girders of the Bandra-Worli sea link providing a counterpoint to the expanse of blue water. The cars crossing the sea link were so far away that they looked like toys, but Mallika seemed unusually fascinated by them.

'Think of all those people driving from one place to

another, feeling ever so busy and important,' she said as Darius came to stand next to her. 'From here they look just like ants—completely insignificant. And if they look at us we'll look like ants to them too.'

Darius turned to face her, leaning his back against the balcony railing. There was a slight breeze ruffling her curls, and her eyes sparkled beguilingly as she smiled up at him.

'It seems to please you,' he said, laughing as he lifted a hand to tuck a stray curl neatly behind her ear. 'The insignificance of humanity in general and the two of us in particular.'

Mallika laughed, and her dimples deepened. Darius's fingers trailed to her cheek and he traced the line of her jaw, his thumb rubbing very close to her mouth. She went very still, but her large eyes held not even a hint of alarm as he bent down to brush his lips lightly against hers.

Her lips were soft and tempting, and they parted very slightly against his. He deepened the kiss, his arms going around her to pull her closer to him. She came willingly, her arms twining eagerly around his neck and her slim body fitting perfectly against his. Kissing her felt completely natural and wildly erotic at the same time, and it took a huge effort of will to finally stop.

He hadn't wanted to—it had been a last remnant of sanity that had prevailed before he could get completely carried away. It was too soon, he hardly knew her, and he was going away in three months. There were all kinds of things wrong with the situation. But the feel of her in his arms had been so right that stopping the kiss had been almost physically wrenching.

Mallika swayed slightly as he raised his head, and he put his hands on her arms to steady her.

'Wow,' she said softly, her eyes still slightly unfocussed. Then a sudden realisation of her surroundings seemed to hit her and she stepped back, running a slightly shaky hand through her hair. 'So, anyway,' she said, rushing into speech before he could say anything. 'You should probably look at the flat and…um…make up your mind. Whether you want to rent it or not. I'll wait here for you.'

'Or you could come and look at it with me?' he suggested, reaching out and taking her hand. She looked uncharacteristically flustered, and he could feel her pulse beating wildly in her wrist.

'Yes, of course,' she said, but she disengaged her hand from his before following him into the flat.

For a few seconds Darius wondered if he should ask her what was going on. The kiss had definitely not been unwelcome—he'd felt the desire surging through her body, and the urgency with which she'd returned it. Even afterwards, the way she'd looked at him had made him think that she wanted to take things further.

The change in her had been sudden—maybe she was just more conservative than she'd initially seemed and was trying to cover up her embarrassment. The temptation to repeat the kiss was huge, but Darius didn't want to crowd her.

It didn't take long for him to look the flat over, and he'd come to a decision by the time they were back in the living room.

'I'll take it,' he said. 'Any idea what rent the landlord's asking?'

She quoted a number that was around fifteen per cent lower than what his broker had quoted for the unfurnished flat he'd seen the week before.

'Are you sure?' he asked. 'Not that I'm complaining, but I was told that rents have gone up in the last few months.'

'There's been a market correction,' Mallika acknowledged. 'Not very major, though, and this building was overpriced to begin with. The landlord will be okay with the rent—she's…um…a little particular about the kind of person she gives the flat to.'

Darius looked around the flat. 'Whose is it?'

'Mine,' she said, and as he turned to look at her in surprise, she said, 'My mum bought up some flats in this building when it was still under construction.'

'When you say "bought up some flats"…?'

'Two,' Mallika said hastily. 'She bought two flats—one each for Aryan and me. The rates were lower when the project was first floated.'

Darius's eyebrows flew up. *His* family was reasonably wealthy, but buying a single flat in this building would use up at least half their life's savings. Buying two at a time was as inconceivable as sauntering off and buying a sack full of diamonds because you were getting them at a discount.

'Did she…um…do this kind of thing often?' he asked.

'Not really,' Mallika said, her voice guarded. 'Real estate is expensive.'

But between Aryan and her, they owned six flats in Mumbai, three in Bangalore and a farmhouse in Alibagh. It was a fact she usually tried to keep hidden—this was the first time she had voluntarily told anyone even about the flat they were standing in.

'Did the previous tenants leave just recently?' Darius asked, instinctively changing the topic. 'The flat looks as if someone was living in it until yesterday.'

Mallika shook her head. 'I got it furnished a year ago,' she said. 'Sometimes I just need a place to…to think in.'

'Most people do their thinking in the bathroom,' Darius said drily.

She flushed, wishing she'd kept her mouth shut. It was too much, expecting him to understand when he didn't know the first thing about her.

'I meant to rent it out eventually,' she muttered. 'I guess I got a little carried away, doing up the place.'

'Clearly you have more money than you know what to do with,' he said, sounding amused. 'Why d'you need a job?'

'To keep myself from going crazy,' she said.

And her voice was so serious that Darius felt she actually meant it.

CHAPTER FIVE

'THIS IS SO typical of a government office,' Darius said, glancing at his watch in annoyance. They were waiting in the property office to register his rent agreement— the appointment had been for seven in the morning, but it was already seven-thirty and the clerks hadn't yet turned up.

'It's always like this,' Mallika said, shrugging. 'Do you have morning meetings?'

He shook his head. 'No, but there's a ton of work I need to get done. And I thought I'd get started on the paperwork for my Schengen visa.'

'Stop thinking about it,' Mallika said, sliding down in her uncomfortable-looking moulded plastic chair and leaning her head against the back to look at the ceiling. 'We're here now. Let's talk about stuff until the clerks turn up.'

'What kind of stuff?' Darius asked, giving her an amused look.

Since the kiss in the flat they hadn't seen each other alone—Darius had been travelling, and after he'd come back Mallika had worked from home for a week. They'd agreed on the rental terms over email and, sensing that she needed some space, Darius hadn't suggested that they meet.

He glanced around the rather seedy office, with its broken furniture and *paan* stains on the walls where it had been chewed and spat out. It wasn't exactly romantic, but at least he was with Mallika, and she looked relaxed and pleased to be spending time with him.

"'Of shoes and ships and sealing wax,'" she said dreamily. "'Of cabbages and kings.'"

'*Alice in Wonderland*,' Darius said. 'It's from The Walrus and The Carpenter poem, isn't it?'

'Is it?' she asked. 'My dad used to keep saying it whenever I asked him what he was thinking about. I didn't realise it was a quotation.'

It was the first time she'd spoken about her father, though her mother figured prominently in her conversation, and Darius took it as a good sign. She was still looking up at the ceiling, as if she found something particularly fascinating in the stains and cracks.

'"*Paisa toh haath ka mail hai,*"' she said after a pause. 'My dad used to keep saying that too. "Money is like dirt on one's palms. Here one moment, washed away the next."'

'He piled up one huge mound of it all the same, though, didn't he?' Darius said without thinking.

Luckily Mallika didn't seem offended. 'Actually, he lost money as fast as he made it,' she said, her mouth curving up into a wry grin. 'It was my mum who was the careful one.'

From her tone, it sounded as if she wished she could admire her mum for it, but couldn't quite bring herself to do so.

Sensing his enquiry, even though Darius hadn't said anything, she went on.

'She was into real estate,' she said. 'My mum. She started off as a real estate agent, but when the markets improved and my dad got back some of his capital she started investing in property herself.'

'Impressive,' he said.

She shrugged. 'I don't think she had much of a choice. My dad couldn't think of any way of making money other than the stock market. If she hadn't taken charge we'd have been out on the streets. Aryan and I were little kids when the stock market crash happened.'

'The Harshad Mehta one?' Darius remembered the crash, but it hadn't affected his life at all. His parents' money was all in fixed deposits and blue chip stocks, so the crash had made good dinnertime conversation—nothing else.

'Yes. My dad lost pretty much all the money we had. Not just his own money but his parents' as well. We used to live in my grandmother's flat in Malabar Hill, but she had to sell it and we moved to a tiny place in Kandivali. Even there, he could barely afford to pay the rent.'

'Must have been tough.'

She shook her head. 'It wasn't. When you're kids it doesn't matter, not living at a good address or having a car and a driver. My dad had more time to spend with us, and he made the whole thing seem like an adventure. He'd take us on bus rides to the zoo and to parks, and he'd invent games for the three of us to play… When I look back, it feels like the best time of my life. It was hell for my mum, though.'

It had been years later when she'd realised that her father had had a mild case of bipolar disorder. The whacky, fun Dad she remembered was the persona he'd taken on during his manic phases. When he'd been going through a depressive episode her mother had concealed it from Aryan and her, telling them that their father was busy at work when he'd locked himself up in a room for hours on end.

'Was that when your mum started up with the real estate thing?'

Mallika nodded. 'She'd been brought up in a rich family, but the dowry she brought with her went with everything else during the crash. And she was too proud to ask her parents for anything more.'

'Why real estate?'

'I guess because that was the only business she understood. Her father was a builder in Gujarat, and she knew how the industry worked. In those days there were very few women property brokers, and she was one of the first to figure out that wives play a huge role in deciding on a house. Most brokers ignored them, but whenever my mom met a couple who was trying to buy a house she went out of her way to understand what kind of layouts the woman liked, how big she wanted the kitchen to be. And kids—no one had heard of pester power, but she made sure she told them about the great play area downstairs and the guy who sold cotton candy across the street...'

'She sounds smart,' Darius said, thinking of his own mother. She was smart too, but she'd been a school-teacher—selling anything at all was completely alien to her character.

'Yes...' Mallika sounded a little sad. 'But along the line she forgot to have fun or spend time with her family or relax. All she did was work hard and make money.

And every rupee she made had to either go into the bank or into property or gold. I probably have more gold jewellery than the Queen of Oman, even though I hate every piece of it.'

Darius gave her a quick smile. 'It sounds like a problem lots of women would love to have,' he said.

Mallika immediately wondered if she'd sounded too self-obsessed, too demanding and needy. It was difficult to explain the various things that had gone wrong in her family without mentioning stuff that she'd rather not talk about. Which begged the question—why the heck had she started moaning about her parents in the first place?

Giving herself a rapid mental slap, she straightened up.

'You're right,' she said. 'Perhaps some day I'll melt all the stuff down and make a dinner set out of it. I've always wanted to eat off a gold plate.'

'Or give it away to charity?' he suggested.

Mallika shook her head with a laugh. 'There's too much of my mum in me to actually give it *all* away. I do the usual annual donations to charities, and to a couple of religious trusts, but not much more.'

Used to people who claimed to do a lot more for society than they actually did, Darius found Mallika refreshingly upfront. He did a fair amount of volunteering, and he supported a small NGO financially as well, but it wasn't something he talked about much. He was beginning to understand the differences between them. Mallika craved stability, structure and security, whereas he longed for adventure, risk and new experiences that pushed boundaries and frontiers.

'What about *your* family?' Mallika was asking. 'What are *they* like?'

Darius grinned. 'They're a bunch of lunatics,' he said. 'Each one's nuttier than the next. Look—I think someone's actually arrived to open up the office.'

He was right—a surly clerk in a bright magenta sari was making a big show of opening a counter and ignoring the people who'd been queuing up for over forty-five minutes waiting for her.

Registering the agreement took around forty minutes—the last step involved putting their thumbprints onto the documents before signing them, and Darius grimaced as the clerk held out a stamp pad with purple ink to him.

'I thought you just took an electronic thumbprint?' he asked.

The clerk gave him a steely look. 'It's part of the procedure, sir,' she said severely.

Mallika suppressed a little giggle. Darius's thumb was now covered with bright purple ink, and he was looking at it with the kind of horror people usually reserved for maggots and slugs.

'Here, let me help,' she said, taking a pack of cleansing tissues out of her bag.

Darius eyed the packet. 'What're those?' he asked, clearly deeply suspicious of anything in pink packaging.

'Make-up-removing tissues,' Mallika said, taking his hand and beginning to rub the ink off his thumb.

They were out of the office and halfway down the dingy stairs, and there was a curious intimacy in the situation. Mallika took her time, her mouth puckering as she concentrated on getting the ink off. Darius stood still and watched her. The temptation to pull her close and kiss her was immense, but they were in a very public place—and already they'd attracted curious looks from a couple of people.

'Thanks,' he said, once she was done with scrubbing his hand. 'Mallika, the other day in the flat...'

Mallika cringed inwardly. She'd behaved stupidly at the flat, and she knew it. She was very thankful Darius had left the topic alone so far—the reason for her behaviour was solid enough, only it was so incredibly embarrassing that she didn't want to talk about it.

'Yes?' she said.

'Did I upset you? Because you've been a little...different ever since.'

'I wasn't expecting it,' she said. 'And I've been feeling a little awkward—I'm sorry.'

She looked up at him, and for a second Darius forgot what he'd been going to say as he looked into her lovely brown eyes.

'I'm sorry if you think I crossed a professional line,' he said after a bit. 'I kissed you on impulse—I wasn't thinking straight.'

'I'm told that the best kisses happen on impulse,' she said, so solemnly that he burst out laughing.

'Really? Who told you that?'

Mallika shrugged. 'I've forgotten,' she said. 'Anyway, whoever it was, they definitely would know more about it than me.'

Darius gave her a curious look. She didn't come across as being prudish or inexperienced—maybe she meant that her previous lovers hadn't been impulsive.

There was a little pause as they walked out of the building. Mallika was looking straight ahead, her lips pressed tightly together. Embarrassing or not, she'd have to tell him if she didn't want a repeat of what had happened in the flat.

They'd agreed to go back to the office together in Darius's car, and Mallika waited till they were safely inside before she said, 'It was the first time.'

He looked puzzled, as well he might—there had been enough of a pause for him to start thinking of something totally different—like national debt, or the future of the economy. Still, Mallika couldn't help feeling peeved at his not understanding immediately. She'd had to muster up a fair bit of courage to say it the first time, and having to repeat it was just piling on the embarrassment.

'It was the first time anyone had kissed me,' she announced, adding firmly, 'I'm warning you—if you laugh I'm going to have to kill you.'

It didn't look as if there was any danger of his laughing—his eyes widened slightly, and he switched the car engine off.

'You mean—ever?'

'Ever,' she said, wishing he wouldn't stare at her as if she was an alien with three heads and a beak. India was still pretty conservative—surely even in Mumbai it wasn't that unusual to have reached the age of twenty-nine without having been kissed?

Except clearly it was, because Darius looked completely gobsmacked. It took him a few seconds to find his voice, and when he did all he said was, 'Does that mean that you're…a…?'

'A virgin?' Feeling really cross now, Mallika said, 'Yes, it does. And I'm surprised you're asking. What kind of person would have sex and not kiss the person that they're…um…'

'Having sex with?' Darius supplied helpfully.

She glared at him, though that was exactly what she'd wanted to say. 'Anyway, so that was why I was feeling awkward,' she said. 'Can we go now?'

'In a minute,' Darius said, and then he leaned across and kissed her again.

Given that this was the second time it had happened, she should have been better prepared. But the kiss was so different from the first that she was left completely stunned. His lips barely grazed hers, and there was something tender, almost reverential in his touch. Unfortunately her long-dormant hormones weren't in the mood to be treated reverentially, and before she knew it her hands had come up to bunch in his shirt and pull him closer.

The kiss suddenly became a lot less tender and a lot more exciting. *Yessss!* her hormones said happily. *Got it right this time. Don't stop!*

She'd have probably gone with the flow, but catching sight of a large and interested audience of street children outside the car had a sudden dampening effect on Mallika. She pulled away abruptly, straightening her hair with unsteady fingers.

'Sorry,' she muttered. 'I got a bit carried away.'

'So did I,' Darius said, his voice amused. 'You have that effect on me.' Then her suddenly horrified expression registered, and he said, 'Are you okay?'

'Your shirt!' Mallika squeaked, and he looked down to survey his once spotless white shirtfront. Not only was it creased where Mallika had grabbed at it, the top button had popped off and her thumb had left purple ink stains all over it.

'I forgot to use the make-up remover on my own hands,' she said ruefully.

He laughed. 'I have a wardrobe full of white shirts,' he said. 'I won't miss this one.'

'I'll get you a new one,' she said. 'I'm so sorry—I'm a complete klutz when I get carried away.'

'Your getting carried away is worth ruining a shirt for,' he said, his smile warm and sexy as he put out a hand to lightly brush her curls back from her face.

She smiled back, though her heart was thumping at twice its normal rate.

'You're pretty amazing—you know that, right?' he said as he leaned across to kiss her again.

The second kiss was less explosive, but it made her feel cherished and incredibly desirable, and it was like stepping out into the sunlight after months of being locked in a cellar. The sensible part of her mind knew perfectly well that Darius was leaving in a few months, and that they had no future together. But somehow it didn't matter—what mattered was the feel of his strong arms around her and his firm lips moving against hers.

When he finally drew away she gave a little moan of protest.

'I know. I feel that way too,' he said regretfully, though his eyes were dancing with amusement. 'But we need to go—we're providing free entertainment to half the street population of Mumbai.'

He was right—the children had gathered closer to the car and were peering in curiously, and Mallika gave a little sigh.

'All right,' she said, though it felt as if she'd been pulled back to earth with a thump.

'There's a bike parked right in front of the car—I'll have to move it,' Darius said, opening the car door and getting out before Mallika could stop him.

The children followed to watch him, offering their help in shrill voices as he wrestled the locked motorcycle a couple of metres down the road. Mallika got out as well. This was the first time she'd seen Darius do anything…well…*physical*, and he was a treat to watch. He must work out often, she thought, admiring the muscles in his back and shoulders as he lifted the bike. And he was strong—the bike weighed a lot more than he did, and he made moving it seem absolutely effortless.

'Today's not my day,' he remarked as he handed the children a handful of loose change and walked back towards the car. 'First ink and then grease.'

Sure enough, his shirt now had a black grease stain on it.

'Give an old woman something…I haven't had a proper meal since yesterday,' a beggar woman whined from the kerb, and Darius gave her the rest of his change before sliding behind the wheel.

'Blessings on you and your pretty one,' the woman called out after them in Hindi. 'May you have a hundred handsome sons!'

'I like the sound of my "pretty one",' Darius said, sounding amused as Mallika spluttered in annoyance. 'Though having a hundred sons sounds a little impractical.'

'I thought you didn't understand Hindi,' she said crossly.

'Oh, I can get by,' he replied. 'Where to now? I need to get out of this shirt before I show up at work, but I can drop you there before going home to change.'

'You could come to my place,' Mallika suggested impulsively. 'It's nearby, and one of Aryan's shirts would fit you.'

Her body was still tingling in the aftermath of the kiss, and she wanted to keep Darius by her side for as long as she could. It was completely out of character for her to suggest such a thing, and it was reckless and spontaneous, but Darius's kiss had opened a door inside her that could not now be closed. She felt free, and she didn't want that feeling to end.

'Are you sure?' Darius asked.

Going to her place implied taking their kiss further, and he wasn't sure at all if that was a good idea. Kissing her had been on his mind for weeks now, and he hadn't been able to resist any longer. But he should have stopped once she'd told him she was a virgin. He had no intention of getting into any kind of long-term relationship—not at this stage in his life—and he couldn't imagine that Mallika was up for a casual fling.

'Sure that the shirt will fit?' Mallika asked, purposely misunderstanding him. 'It will—Aryan's skinnier than you, but he wears his shirts loose.'

She wasn't sure how Aryan would react to her bringing a man home—either he wouldn't even notice or he'd withdraw even further into his shell—but she found she didn't care. Her home had begun to seem like a prison to her. She loved Aryan to bits, and she felt responsible for him, but he seemed to be getting worse, becoming increasingly difficult to manage, and demanding more and more of her time.

The thought of taking Darius home was strangely liberating. She'd spent the last two years of her life mourning her parents and helplessly watching Aryan get worse. Her friends had gone through the usual ups and downs of relationships and heartbreak before settling down, but she'd listened to her ultraconservative mother and steered clear of men. And after the accident she had been so wrapped up in Aryan that she'd had no time for anyone else.

If she hadn't met Darius she probably wouldn't even have realised that she was living a half-life, and every instinct told her to make the most of the time she had with him. With her mother gone, her links with her conservative extended family had weakened, and she didn't really care what they thought of what she did. And right now she wanted to be with Darius more than anything else.

It took them less than ten minutes to reach her apartment complex, and Darius parked in a free spot outside the compound wall.

'Should I wait here?' he asked in a last-ditch attempt to keep his distance.

She shook her head. 'Better come with me,' she said. 'You'll need to try on the shirt. And I'll give you the keys to your flat too. Now that the paperwork's done, and everything, you'll probably want to move in this weekend.'

A neighbour coming out of the building looked a little surprised to see Darius, but Mallika gave her a sweet smile and swept him into the lift without stopping to talk. The neighbour had known her for years and was a notorious gossip. Mallika would bet her last rupee that she'd make an excuse to call or come over in the evening, with the sole purpose of finding out who Darius was.

The lift stopped on the third floor and Darius followed her to the door of her flat. She dug around in her bright blue tote for the keys—while Aryan was at home, there was only around a ten per cent chance of him opening the door if she rang the bell. Mostly, unless he'd ordered something for himself on the internet and was expecting it to be delivered, he didn't bother answering the door.

Mallika used her own keys to let herself in and out, and she'd got duplicates made for the cook and the cleaner.

Darius's clear, warm gaze on her made her fumble a little, but she finally got the door open, flushing a little as she ushered him in. He stopped as he stepped in, looking around the flat in surprise. He'd expected it to be done up in the same way as the flat he was renting—clean lines, lots of light and space. This flat, however, was crammed full of heavy furniture in some kind of dark wood. The upholstery was in shades of brown and maroon, and the oil paintings on the walls were depressing landscapes in dingy colours. Mallika herself seemed to have shrunk a little after stepping into the flat.

'We...um...usually take our shoes off before going into the house,' she said as she pushed the door open, slipping her own flat-soled pumps off and putting them on a rack just inside the door.

It was a common enough rule in conservative house-holds, and Darius gave her an impish wink as he sat down on a bench next to the shoe rack and pulled off his shoes and socks.

'Sorry,' she said. 'My mum used to be very fussy about shoes in the house, and we've stuck to the rule even without her being around to yell at us.'

'It's a sensible rule,' he said, suddenly understand-ing why the house looked the way it did. She'd probably changed nothing after her parents had died.

He knew how much she hated any kind of pitying overture, so he didn't say anything, but his heart went out to her.

'I'll get the shirt—give me a minute,' she said, and went into a little corridor and knocked on Aryan's door.

There was no response, and after a minute she gave an exasperated little huff and went into the kitchen.

There was a little service area beyond the kitchen, and a pile of ironed clothes was lying on top of the washing machine. She took two shirts out of the heap and went back to the living room. Darius was still standing, and she held the shirts out to him.

'Here—one of these should fit,' she said. 'You can change in my room.'

Her room turned out to be at the end of the corridor, and unlike the intensely depressing living room it was painted a bright, clean white, with blue curtains and a turquoise bedspread. It was a cheerful room, and Darius felt a lot better as soon as he stepped into it.

'I'll find you a bag to carry your messed-up shirt in,' Mallika said as she shut the door behind her, and she went across to the small dressing table that occupied one corner of the room. 'Here you go.'

She handed him a medium-sized plastic bag and then went to sit on the bed, her eyes on him. The kiss earlier in the car had left her in a confused, half-aroused state so that she could hardly think straight. All she knew was that she wanted to kiss him again, and his suddenly formal attitude was making her feel so frustrated she could scream.

Darius caught her eye and started undoing the top button of his shirt.

Mallika was mesmerised. She couldn't move. 'Uh… maybe I should leave?' she eventually managed to say, but he laughed mischievously.

Darius continued to unbutton his shirt, a gently teasing smile on his lips, and Mallika knew she couldn't leave now. With a boldness that surprised her she slipped off the bed in one fluid movement and came up to him.

'I can help if you want,' she said softly, her hands going to the buttons of his stained shirt.

In the back of her mind Mallika was aware of a lifetime of duty, responsibility and conservative values. But faced with Darius, this beautiful man with his quiet strength, who challenged her but never tried to control her, she found herself responding with an uncharacteristically coy smile. This wasn't her, but it was the person she wanted to be—even if only for a little while. And it felt good…really good.

Darius stood very still as she undid the first two buttons, her hand slipping under the cloth to slide over his bare chest. Inexperienced she might be, but Mallika was very aware of what she was doing and the effect she was having on him. The height difference between them was only a few inches, and she leaned up to press her lips against his, her hands still busy with the buttons. Her tongue lightly teased his mouth, and finally that proved too much for Darius's self-control.

With a muttered oath, he pulled her into his arms, his mouth hard and demanding against hers. His shirt had fallen open, all buttons finally undone, and Mallika could feel his heart pounding under velvety hair-roughened skin.

Without quite knowing how she'd got there Mallika found herself lying on the bed, pinned under his heavy body as he began to kiss his way down her throat. Her hands knotted in his hair and she arched her body to get as close to his as she could without actually breaking skin. Her own clothes were in disarray, her top having ridden up to expose most of her torso, and the feel of his bare skin against hers was indescribably good.

They were probably a nanosecond away from having hot, messy sex on the bed when the sound of a door closing in another part of the flat made Darius jerk away from her.

'Damn, I'm so sorry,' he said.

His eyes were still hooded and a little unfocused as he groaned under his breath and wrapped his arms around Mallika to hold her tightly against his body.

'Bad timing,' he said softly as he dropped a kiss onto her forehead. 'I wish I'd met you a couple of years earlier, Mallika, before I decided to leave India.'

'You could delay going a little,' Mallika said, but she stopped trying to get the rest of his clothes off. She could feel the moment slipping away and she couldn't bear it. 'Or we could just be together until you leave.'

'It's not fair to you,' he said gently. 'Not that I wouldn't love to take this to…to a logical conclusion. I shouldn't have kissed you to begin with, and what happened right now was pretty inexcusable.'

Feeling frustrated, and a little hurt, Mallika sighed. He was right about their timing being completely off, and Mallika wished desperately that she *had* met him a few years earlier. Not that she was in the market for a serious relationship either, but at least they'd have had time to work something out. At least she could have explored all the new sensations and desires that were currently flooding her system. But it looked as if she was going to have to imagine where they might take her instead.

'Go latch the door and put on one of the shirts,' she said, pushing him lightly away.

He groaned reluctantly but got up, giving her an

opportunity to admire his perfectly toned torso as he shrugged off the shirt and put on a clean one. She'd been right—Darius was broader built and more muscular than Aryan, but the shirt fitted perfectly. And the colour suited him. So far, she'd seen Darius only in white or cream formal shirts. This one was a dark blue, and set off his golden skin and jet-black hair perfectly.

'Looking good, Mr Mistry,' she said as he bundled up his old shirt and shoved it into the plastic bag. 'Time for a cup of coffee before you go?'

Darius nodded and Mallika slid off the bed and headed for the kitchen, hastily rearranging her clothes into some semblance of normal.

'Black or with milk?' she asked.

'Black, but with plenty of sugar,' he said.

He took a minute before following her out—his body had reacted with indecent haste to her kisses and he wanted to be sure he was fit to be seen before he left the room. Once he was sure he had everything under control, he tucked the shirt in, gave himself a cursory look in the mirror and strode out.

Mallika was tapping a foot nervously on the floor as she spooned instant coffee powder into two mugs. Her frustration at having to stop was turning into an irritation with everything around her—especially Aryan, who'd disturbed them by slamming his door shut.

'D'you want to grab something to eat before we leave?' she asked Darius when he walked into the kitchen.

It wasn't food he was thinking about just then, but he shrugged. 'A sandwich or something,' he said. 'I'm not particularly hungry.'

She handed him his coffee and went to the fridge.

'I'm sure I can figure something out. The cook will have made lunch for Aryan...I'll just need to see if there's enough for all of us.'

'Mally, do you know where my camera is?'

Darius had built up a mental picture of Aryan, and the reality was so different from the weedy, sallow-looking youth he'd imagined that he blinked in surprise. The resemblance between brother and sister was so close that they could have been twins if not for the obvious differences of gender and age. If anything, Aryan was better-looking than Mallika, and other than his skin being a little pale there was nothing to indicate that he hadn't been out of doors in months.

Mallika had turned at the sound of his voice, and she said curtly, 'It's in my room. And you're not getting it back until you promise to stop taking photos from your window.'

'I promise,' he said. 'Can I have it back now?'

'I'll tell you in the evening,' she said. 'Say hello to Darius, Aryan.'

Aryan's brow furrowed a little as he turned.

'Hello, Darius,' he said slowly, and it was difficult to tell if he was being sarcastic or not. His brown eyes, disconcertingly like Mallika's, flicked over Darius, stopping a little to take in the shirt.

'I lent him one of your shirts,' Mallika said. 'His got ruined by ink and grease—long story. Have you had lunch?'

'Fruit and some milk,' Aryan said. 'There were only oily *parathas* for lunch.'

'Those'll do for us,' Mallika said, locating the *parathas*

and sliding them onto two plates with a little heap of pickle on each. 'Here you go, Darius.'

Darius took the plate. Their hands touched briefly, and a slight blush suffused Mallika's face. Aryan gave her a thoughtful look, but he didn't say anything.

Mallika looked up at him. 'Did you get any work done today, Aryan?' she asked.

'Lots,' he said, stretching like a cat, his mouth curving into a boyish smile that was surprisingly charming. 'The market's very active today.'

'Hmm, I saw the alerts,' Mallika said as she finished her last *paratha*. 'Be careful, though, it'll be very volatile until the elections. Shall we go, Darius? Venkat's probably tearing his hair out—I was supposed to submit a report to him before lunch.'

Aryan watched them leave, an indefinable expression in his eyes. There was clearly a lot going on beneath the surface with Mallika's brother that Darius could only guess at.

'See you around,' Darius said as he brushed past him to get to the door. 'I'll get the shirt cleaned and sent back to you in a couple of days.'

'See you,' he echoed.

His voice was perfectly cordial, though Darius got the impression that Aryan was happy to see him go. It was an odd set-up, and he felt desperately sorry for Mallika, living in that depressing flat with only her reclusive brother for company.

'Aryan works?' Darius asked as they got into the car. He didn't want to talk about what had just happened between them, and felt that Mallika was thinking the same.

'Stock-trading,' Mallika said. 'He inherited the knack from my father and he's doing quite well. Unlike my dad, he knows how to take calculated risks, so he makes money.'

'And your dad?' Darius said eventually.

She shrugged. 'Made a fortune one day—lost it the next. He let his gambling instincts take over too often.'

There hadn't been any photos in the house, Darius realised suddenly. That was what had seemed out of place. The flat was like a museum—all that expensive heavy furniture and dark draperies—with no personal touches at all. No photographs, no tacky souvenirs from foreign trips, no sign that anyone actually *lived* there.

'What did you think of him?' Mallika was asking. 'Aryan, I mean. It's been a while since he met anyone. He doesn't go out, and the only people who visit us have known him for years. I was wondering how he comes across to someone who's met him for the first time.'

'He didn't talk much,' Darius said cautiously. 'It's not that uncommon to be a bit of a hermit at that age, is it?'

'"A bit of a hermit"?' she repeated, and laughed shortly. 'That's a good description.'

He got the sense that she wanted to say more, but she seemed to think better of it and began talking about work instead. Darius felt a strange sense of frustration—not all of it physical. There was something elusive about Mallika…a quicksilver quality that made him feel he was never quite sure of where he was with her.

The admission that he was the first man she'd ever kissed had shaken him up—it was the first indication he'd got that she felt more for him than she'd shown. As for his own feelings—he knew he was already in way too deep to walk away at this point. In addition to wanting her so badly that it hurt, he needed to talk to her, find out what made her tick.

CHAPTER SIX

'NOT THIS WEEKEND. Aryan needs me around,' Mallika said.

She'd tried talking to Aryan again about getting help—it was eight months now since he'd last stepped out of the flat—but she hadn't got anywhere. And he'd been even more distant since he'd met Darius, talking even less than usual and not coming out of his room except for meals. She was really worried about him—afraid he would become so reclusive that she would lose him completely.

'I really want to see you,' Darius said, his voice dropping an octave.

She felt a pleasurable heat curling through her body. And this was in reaction to just his *voice*. A mental image of him shirtless and super-hot intruded, and she squirmed.

'I want to see you too,' she whispered back. 'It's just that this weekend is a bit…tough. I need to figure a few things out.'

As she put the phone down she noticed Aryan at the door, looking at her. It was impossible to gauge how much he'd overheard, and he didn't say anything—just walked off to the dining table.

A surge of annoyance left her cheeks warm and her pulse racing—she badly wanted to meet Darius, and Aryan was one of the main reasons she'd said no. But it seemed a rather pointless sacrifice when it didn't seem to be helping him.

She obsessed over it for a while, before she came to a decision. Her aunt wouldn't mind coming down and being with Aryan for a bit—heaven knew she deserved to have a life of her own. For a minute she wondered what her mother would have thought of her decision and her nerve almost failed her. Her mother had been courageous and independent, but she'd also been rigidly conventional—which was partly why she'd ended up being deeply unhappy all her life. She'd have hated the thought of what Mallika was about to do. But she was gone anyway, and Mallika had her own life to live and her own choices to make.

Picking up her phone, she typed out a quick text.

Are you still free this weekend? Might be able to meet you on Saturday.

Her text arrived in the nick of time—Darius was just about to promise an elderly aunt that he'd drive her to visit a friend who lived around thirty kilometres away.

'Next Saturday instead,' he told his aunt firmly.

The last time he'd driven Auntie Freny to meet a friend she'd insisted on leaving home at nine in the morning, and had subsequently proceeded to party till three the *next* morning.

'*Dikra*, this time you can have a drink too,' Auntie Freny said cajolingly.

Darius promptly felt as if he was six again, being promised a chocolate if he was good.

'Last time, *ni*, you had to drive, no? This time we can stay overnight—just pack some clothes.'

'Next Saturday,' Darius said, and gave his aunt an affectionate hug.

'Some girl you're going to meet—don't think I don't know.'

His aunt made a surprisingly nimble grab for his phone, and Darius managed to whisk it away only just in time.

Balked of her fun, Freny shook her head at him sorrowfully. 'Never do I get to meet these girls. Get married and settle down, *dikra*, this is no time for flirting and having fun. Our race is dying out! I went to the Parsi *panchayat* last week and...'

'And they told you that unless I got married and fathered fifteen children I'd be responsible for the end of the Parsis?'

Aunt Freny gave him an exasperated look. 'No, I met an old friend with a really nice daughter who'd be perfect for you. If you just met her once you'd give up this crazy idea of travelling around in all kinds of strange places, away from your family. Should I call my friend?'

'Thanks, but no thanks,' Darius said firmly. 'I'm perfectly capable of finding a girlfriend of my own if I want one.'

'Freny, he doesn't *want* to marry and settle down,' his mother said tartly as she walked into the room. 'If he did, he wouldn't want to go traipsing across the world like this.' She caught Darius's suddenly stricken look and added in a gentler tone, 'Relax, I'm not trying to make you feel guilty. You've done everything you can for this family, and you deserve a few adventures for yourself.'

Finding something to wear for a date when you possessed a sum total of zero remotely suitable outfits shouldn't have been difficult, but it was.

Mallika grimaced as she surveyed her clothes. She had several shelves of cotton tunics that she teamed with jeans when she went out to indulge her photography hobby, two formal business suits, a couple of silk *churidaar kameez*, and half a dozen saris. Dozens of loose cotton T-shirts...

Even the 'remotely suitable' outfits were beginning to look unusable—one of the tops had a mark on it, and the other two hung loose on her slim frame. Evidently she'd lost weight and not realised it.

Beginning to feel a little desperate, she took everything out of the wardrobe, in the hope that something suitable would surface. Buying new clothes to go out with Darius would be taking the concept of trying too hard to a completely different level...

Perhaps she could wear a silk *kameez* over jeans and pretend that she was going for an arty look.

At the back of the wardrobe, a little patch of flame-coloured matt silk caught her eye. *Ah, right.* That was the dress that an old college friend had given her, evidently not realising that Mallika never wore dresses or skirts.

Tugging the dress from its cellophane wrapping, she shook it out and held it against herself. There was a reason why she avoided anything that showed her legs—there was a narrow, but very visible scar from a bicycle accident that ran up her left leg from mid-calf to knee.

'If it scares him off it's probably a good thing,'

she muttered to herself as she pulled the dress on and smoothed it over her hips.

It should have looked hideous. The colour was anything but subtle, and it was a while since she'd last worn a dress. But the fabric clung softly to her curves, outlining the soft swell of her breasts and emphasising her perfect waist. The hem was asymmetrical, and it hid part of the scar—but she found the scar itself was nowhere as scary as she remembered it being. Her legs were long and shapely, and the scar was barely noticeable.

The dress was probably not suitable for a simple date, but once she'd seen how she looked she didn't feel like taking it off.

'You're looking nice,' Aryan informed her as she stepped out of her room.

Her eyes flew up to his in surprise. She hadn't expected him to come out of his room to see her off. Still less had she expected him to notice what she was wearing.

Feeling the excitement drain out of her, she said tentatively, 'Thanks. Um…are you sure you'll be okay with *mausiji*?'

He nodded, and when she didn't look convinced gave her a crooked smile. 'I'm alone at home when you go to work,' he reminded her. 'Go ahead—I'll be fine today.'

Aryan probably hadn't intended it, but she felt inordinately guilty as she stepped out of the flat. She did her best to work from home whenever she could, but she did end up having to go to the office at least two, sometimes three days a week. Aryan never liked being left alone in the flat, and ever since she'd changed jobs he'd been more on edge—staying in his room and skipping meals if she wasn't around to force him to eat.

Darius was waiting in his car at the end of the lane, and she half ran the rest of the way to reach him.

He leaned across and unlocked the door, giving her a quizzical smile as she slid in, half out of breath. 'Are the Feds after you?' he asked.

She laughed. 'No—worse, I have the snoopiest neighbours in the universe. So, what are we doing today?'

He'd planned lunch and a movie, but one look at Mallika in her flame-coloured dress had driven everything out of his head—all he could think of was taking her home and making slow, delicious love to her.

'Whatever you want,' he said slowly. 'I've booked tickets for a movie, and a table at a restaurant. But most of all I want to talk to you. We left a lot of things unfinished the last time we met.'

His eyes met hers, and it was as if she could read what he'd been thinking a second ago.

'You've moved into the Parel flat, haven't you?' she asked, and he nodded. 'And have you managed to set up your home theatre system yet?'

He nodded again, and she broke into a smile so bright and alluring that he could hardly tear his eyes away from her face.

'Let's go there then,' she said. 'Watch an old movie, order takeaway…talk.'

'Right,' he said, his throat suddenly dry. 'Sounds like a plan.'

Predictably, watching a movie was the last thing on their minds as they tumbled into the flat fifteen minutes later. Darius had pretty much broken every speed limit in town, getting them there, and they were barely inside the flat before Mallika was in his arms, kissing him so eagerly that it took his breath away.

'Slow down,' he said softly, smoothing her hair away from her face. 'We have all the time in the world. And I really do think we should talk.'

It took everything he had not to whisk her straight into the bedroom, but it was important that they laid some ground rules before taking things further.

She sighed and pulled away from him. 'What's there to talk about?' she asked. 'You're leaving in a few months and I'm stuck here.'

'I know,' he said. 'Logically, we should stay away from each other—but that's not happening, is it?' It looked as if she wanted to interrupt, but he went on, 'It's mostly my fault—I've been trying to convince you to meet me. If you want me to, I'll stop.'

'I don't want you to stop,' Mallika said, her voice low. 'Look, I can't commit to a long-term thing either, but I haven't felt like this about anyone ever before. I haven't wanted to do this with anyone before. Maybe it's just physical attraction, but I…I dream about you. And when I'm with you I can't seem to stop myself from…from…'

Touching you, she wanted to say. *Kissing you and wanting to make love to you all night long.* The words didn't come, though—and already she'd said more than she'd meant to.

Darius's expression had changed. Maybe he thought she was throwing herself at him. She quickly tried to dispel the thought.

'I can't marry while I still have Aryan to look after,' she said. 'Until I met you I used to stay away from men and concentrate on work. It was much easier that way.

Only with you I've not been able to stick to the rules I made for myself.'

Mallika took a deep breath. She'd never had such a conversation with a man before, and she had to screw up her courage to get the next words out.

'So I was thinking—maybe I should just forget about the rules for a bit. Do what *I* want for once—with someone who wants it just as much as I do.'

Darius leaned closer to her, capturing both her hands in his. 'Mallika, I don't want to take advantage,' he said. 'I'm crazy for you, but the last thing I want to do is hurt you in any way.'

'You won't,' she said, her eyes meeting his steadily. 'I know you'll leave, and I'm okay with it. I just…' Her voice quivered a bit, but she steadied it with a visible effort. 'I haven't really been able to let go and do what I want. *Ever.* When I was in school and college I was studying hard all the time, because that was the way my mother wanted it. Even when I started working I stayed away from parties and men. She was trying to protect me because she'd had such a tough life herself. By the time I figured out that the world wasn't that bad after all, she was dead. And I had Aryan to look after.'

Darius's eyes were sympathetic now, and she felt she couldn't bear it.

'While you're here, let's be together,' she said, making her voice as upbeat and cheerful as possible. 'And once you need to go we'll separate—with no regrets. How does that sound?'

'Like the last bit's going to be damn tough,' Darius said honestly. 'I'm finding it difficult enough to be objective right now. I don't know what it'll be like three months from now.'

'If we're lucky it'll wear off by then,' she said.

He had to laugh. 'If we're lucky,' he repeated, tracing a line down the side of her face with one hand and watching her quiver in response. 'But—just so that you know—even if we're perfect together I'm not going to stay. I need a clean break from my current life, and that's important for me. More important than anything else.'

'Relax, I get that,' she murmured. 'If you like we'll get the legal team to draft a set of disclaimers for you! I'm not looking for a happy ending, here—just a few weeks of fun.'

'Right,' he said.

There was an awkward moment while they stared at each other, both unsure of what to do next, then Darius muttered something and swept her into his arms, his lips hot and insistent against hers. Mallika melted against him, but a few minutes later, as his hands went to the zip on her dress, she made a little sound of protest and Darius pulled back.

'Are you okay?' he asked, his mouth against her throat.

She nodded her head. 'Yes,' she said decisively. 'Just go a little slower. I'm...nervous.'

The admission shook him more than he would have cared to admit and he changed his touch, skimming his hands over her skin as gently as if she was made of spun glass.

It was only when she made a little sound in her throat and pressed her hips hard against his that he let his lips become a little more urgent, his hands more demanding...

Much later, Mallika raised her head lazily from Darius's shoulder and surveyed the room. Her dress lay in a tangled heap near the foot of the bed, next to his jeans, and the rest of their clothing was strewn around the room. It was a miracle that they'd made it to the bed and not ended up making love on the living room sofa or on the floor.

'That was good,' she said.

'Just *good*? I must be losing my touch,' he murmured, running a finger lightly down her arm. She shivered in reaction and he grinned, twisting her around to kiss her. 'Did I hurt you?' he asked, more seriously.

She shook her head. 'I'm a little sore, but I guess that's to be expected. And I hate to spoil the mood, but I'm starving after all that exercise. Any chance of getting something to eat?'

'We'll have to order in,' Darius said. 'The sum total of food available in this house is one apple and a box of biscuits.'

'I'll take the apple,' she said, turning and burrowing closer to him.

'I have some takeaway menus in the kitchen,' Darius said. What do you feel like eating?'

'I'm not sure,' Mallika said with a sigh. Lying in Darius's arms felt so good she wouldn't move at all if her stomach weren't rumbling.

'Did you live here ever, Mallika?' he asked. 'Before you decided to rent the flat out?'

The place had a sense of having been lived in, despite its pristine state.

'I wanted to move here when my parents died,' she said. 'Our old place reminds me of them every minute I'm in the flat. But Aryan wasn't keen, and now I can't leave him there by himself.'

'That's understandable,' he said.

There was a brief pause as Mallika cuddled up closer

to him and nibbled playfully at his shoulder. She responded enthusiastically when he pulled her in for a hard kiss, but after a bit twisted away from him.

'I'm really, really hungry,' she said. 'Can we order food first?'

Darius groaned and picked up the first of the menus. 'Here you go,' he said. 'I can see I'm much lower in your priority list than lunch.'

Mallika took the menu and gave him a conciliatory little kiss. 'You're *much* more important than lunch,' she assured him. 'I just want to get lunch out of the way so that I can concentrate on you.'

The thought of her concentrating only on him made it difficult for Darius to think straight, but he leaned back and watched Mallika as she went through the menu.

'*Tandoori roti, daal tadka* and *aloo jeera*,' she said. 'What about you?'

'I think I'll have the chicken *sagawala*,' he said, mentioning the first thing he'd noticed on the menu. 'Or, no—you're vegetarian. I'll have the same stuff you're having.'

'I'm okay with you ordering chicken as long as I don't have to eat it,' Mallika said. 'But it's *saagwala*—not *sagawala.*'

Darius frowned. 'What's the difference?'

'*Saagwala* means that it's made in a spinach sauce,' she explained patiently. '*Sagawala* means that the chicken is a blood relative.'

'Seriously?'

'Seriously.'

He looked impressed. 'There's more to this speaking Hindi thing than meets the eye,' he said. 'Maybe you should give me Hindi lessons.'

'Maybe I should,' she said, dimpling as she tossed the menu back to him and went to get a glass of water.

Darius used his cell phone to order lunch, and once he was done wandered back to the bedroom. He lay down and stared at the ceiling. In spite of it being Mallika's first time, the sex had been mind-blowing, and he could hardly stop a goofy grin from spreading across his face at the thought of how good it had been.

Mallika came back into the room a few minutes later, still swathed in the bed sheet. She perched on his side of the bed and looked at him thoughtfully. Darius was sitting up now, his bare chest on display as he gave her a slow smile—and he looked so heartbreakingly perfect that for an instant she forgot the lines she'd been rehearsing in the kitchen.

Impulsively, she leaned across and kissed him, but pulled away when he tried to take her into her arms. Losing her head once a day was enough—it had been amazing, unforgettable, but now she needed to be sensible.

'This is going to be complicated,' she said. 'We should talk.'

CHAPTER SEVEN

'I AGREE,' DARIUS SAID. 'I think ground rules are a very good idea.'

'So that we don't end up making a mess of things,' Mallika continued. 'I mean, you'll be going away, so it doesn't matter so much for you, but I don't want to have to deal with unnecessary gossip.' She thought for a moment, and went on, 'Plus it'll be difficult for me if Aryan finds out. He's very fragile right now—even more so than usual.'

'We don't need to tell him,' Darius said, reacting to the last sentence first. Her expression changed and he added hastily, 'Or anyone else. What's next?'

He looked so tempting, standing there with his shirt still partly unbuttoned and his hair rumpled after making love, that Mallika felt like abandoning the list of rules and going back to bed with him.

Sighing, she turned away and walked to the window. 'Gossip is only part of it,' she said. 'We should probably be careful not to…um…get too close—like talk about our lives too much and all that. Keep it limited to the physical stuff.'

Darius nodded again, a little more slowly this time. What she said made sense, but it made him think that she was perhaps more emotionally affected than she said she was. It sounded as if she was trying to build up walls so that she didn't get hurt when he left.

'What else?' he asked, beginning to wonder if this had all been a huge mistake.

He was a lot more experienced than her, and he should have foreseen the complications that would occur if they slept together. He couldn't get tangled up in something that would make him question his travels. He needed this…he *deserved* this—it had been his goal for so many years and now it was within touching distance. He wouldn't give it up—not again.

'We should…um…be together only in the evenings,' she said. 'I'll come to you.'

That would set some boundaries, she thought. Ensure that she didn't throw herself at him at all hours. And she'd make sure she went to him only on the days that she'd been working from home, so Aryan wasn't alone for more than a few hours.

He nodded again, and she said. 'Just one more thing. I have a lot of stuff going on right now, so while I'd love to meet you as often as you want to it probably won't be possible.'

This was beginning to sound a bit clinical, thought Darius. He understood that Mallika was only trying to protect herself, and goodness knew the rules certainly worked in his favour, but it made him feel concerned that she had already got in over her head.

'Problems with Aryan?' Darius asked, and his voice was so gentle that Mallika felt suddenly very close to tears.

'Yes,' she said. 'He doesn't like me leaving him at home and going out.'

Darius moved to stand behind her, his arms coming around her to pull her gently against him. He would agree to the rules, of course, but he would have to stay on his guard. After all, rules could always be broken.

'Maybe I could help?' he suggested. 'If nothing else, I could take your mind off everything that's bothering you.'

Mallika turned abruptly and buried her face in his chest. 'It isn't so simple,' she said, her voice muffled against his shirt.

'It could be,' he said, his breath stirring her hair. 'Think about it.'

'I should go now,' she said, without looking up. It's getting late and Aryan's alone. My aunt will have left by now.'

For a few seconds Darius felt like telling her that Aryan was a grown man and capable of taking care of himself for a few hours. But he bit the words back. Mallika clearly felt responsible for her brother, and making snide remarks about him wouldn't help matters. Also, he trusted her judgement—if she said her brother wasn't fit to be left alone for long periods she was probably right.

But he was feeling incredibly frustrated—Mallika had got to him in a way no woman had before, and her determination to stay emotionally unattached bothered him more than he would have expected.

'I'll drop you home,' he said, but she shook her head again.

'I'll take a cab.'

'Stop being stubborn about it,' he said. 'Even if someone sees us, we can tell them you're my landlady.'

She nodded obediently, and Darius tipped her face

up so that she was forced to look right into his laughing eyes.

'Come on, landlady,' he said teasingly. 'Let's get you home.'

Perhaps it would have been easier if Darius had taken her rules at face value, Mallika thought a few weeks later. She slipped into Darius's flat almost every alternate evening, and the sex was as hot and passionate as it had been the first time. But Darius didn't seem content with that—she'd expected that he would stay away from her when they weren't actually sleeping together, but he was doing quite the opposite.

'People know that we're friends,' he said. 'It'll seem far more suspicious if I stop talking to you at work than if we continue to hang out together.'

And so, in public, he'd assumed the role of a friend—one who wanted to spend as much time with her as possible. Every couple of days he'd call to suggest meeting up for coffee or a movie—if she said no he'd laugh and suggest an alternative date. Or he'd bully her into admitting she needed a break and take her out anyway.

Once he'd bought tickets for a stand-up comedy show and told Venkat that she needed to leave work early to participate in a personality development exercise.

Venkat had asked suspiciously, 'What's wrong with her personality?'

He'd said, 'Her sense of humour could do with some work—she takes life way too seriously.'

And Venkat, who wouldn't have recognised a joke if it had walked up and hit him on the nose, had agreed with him and forced her to go.

Another time he'd booked both of them onto a heritage walk across the old parts of South Mumbai, which had ended at an open-air music festival at the Gateway of India. The music had been a crazy jumble of jazz, blues, fusion and rock, and Mallika had had the time of her life.

Afterwards, they'd wandered through Colaba and had dinner at a little tucked-away Lebanese café. They'd talked for hours and hours about music and travel and books, and hadn't realised how late it was until they'd been the last people in the café, with the owner waiting patiently for them to pay their bill and leave.

When she'd got home Aryan had been waiting for her, his eyes large and accusing in his pale face, and she'd resolved never to stay out so late again.

The next few times Darius had asked her out she'd made excuses and stayed at home, playing Scrabble with Aryan, or just sitting in his room with a book while he pored over his laptop screen.

Today, Darius was on the phone insisting she get up at this unearthly hour in the morning to go with him to Sewri. A flock of migratory flamingos stopped at the Sewri mudflats for a few weeks every year on their way from Siberia, and Darius was appalled to hear that she'd lived in Mumbai for her entire life and never seen them.

'Darius, I can't,' she protested. 'I've just woken up, and I need to get breakfast for Aryan. And I need to go to my Alibagh house for a few hours in the afternoon. I can't come.'

And I can't be with you and pretend to be friends without wanting much more, she said silently to herself. It was time she put her foot down and made sure they stuck to the rules. She was new at this, and she could feel herself starting to fall for him, to rely on him being a part of her life. She didn't want to get hurt, and of course there was Aryan to consider.

'I'll stop at a café and fetch something for Aryan's breakfast,' Darius said easily. 'And we'll be done with the flamingos by ten—I'll drop you to the ferry after that.'

'I don't want to leave Aryan alone for that long,' she said. 'My aunt can't come over today—she's got a *puja* prayer ritual to go to. And I'm a little tired.'

She'd woken up with a bad headache, and the thought of the Alibagh trip was depressing. The little beach villa was where her parents had died—she'd not been able to bring herself either to sell it or rent it out, and it had been lying vacant for the last two years. It had been repainted after the accident, and there was a caretaker who kept the house clean and tended the lawn, but she'd visited it only four times in the last two years. Now there was a leakage problem and she had to go.

'We can go tomorrow, then,' Darius said. 'Or next week, if you like.'

Mallika sighed, and then said abruptly, 'Darius, why are you doing this?'

'Doing what?' he asked innocently.

'You know what I mean,' Mallika said.

She got up and closed the door to her room, to make sure that Aryan couldn't overhear her.

'Look, we're doing what we said we would—having a fling before you go to Alaska or Mongolia or wherever. But you're also doing this "just good friends" routine. I'm not sure if it's fooling anyone, and it's definitely confusing the hell out of *me*. It just…doesn't make sense.'

'It does to me,' he said. 'I really like you. I like being with you—in bed and out of it. And, maybe I'm wrong, but it feels like you don't have any close friends—not people you can be yourself with.'

'So you feel *sorry* for me?'

She probably hadn't meant to sound bitter, but it came out that way and Darius winced. He hadn't wanted to have this conversation so soon—and definitely not over the phone. What she'd said about never having had a chance to have fun and do what she wanted had struck a chord with him. He'd never had the kind of problems she had, but he understood the need to break loose and he'd been doing his best to help.

Quite apart from that was the fact that he actually loved every minute he spent with her—but he tried not to think about that too much. He knew that their spending time together like this was dancing on the edge of what their rules allowed, but somehow he couldn't stop himself.

'Not sorry, exactly,' he said. 'I just think that you're young and you have your whole life ahead of you—it's a little early to be cooping yourself up at home and only coming out when you need to go to work. You said it yourself—you want to go out and have fun, do all the things you missed doing when you were younger.'

'I might have said it, but it's not practical to think only about myself,' she said. 'I have a brother with problems, remember?'

'I know,' Darius said.

She didn't mention Aryan often, but he had now got a fair idea of what she was dealing with there. He gritted his teeth before plunging ahead.

'But I don't think you can solve his problems by locking yourself away as well. He needs professional help, and the sooner you get it for him the better it'll be for both of you.'

'Perhaps *I* need professional help as well, then,' Mallika said. 'Because I can't see my way to dragging him to a doctor when he refuses to go. And I can't stop caring about him or looking after him.'

'There's always a way out,' Darius said. 'It's just not obvious because you're so closely involved.'

'Maybe I don't want a way out,' she said softly, the hopelessness of the entire situation striking her anew. 'I'm not like you, Darius—I can't just walk away from my family without a backward glance.'

There was a long pause, and then Darius asked, 'Is that what you think I'm doing?'

'Well, isn't it?' she countered hotly. He had pressed her buttons and now her blood was up. She was spoiling for a fight. 'Your parents are old, and there's your grandmother, and your aunt—you're just leaving them to fend for themselves, aren't you?'

'My sister's here,' he said, wondering why he was even bothering to justify himself.

He hadn't talked to Mallika about his family much—their rules forbade it, after all—so it wasn't surprising that she was jumping to all the wrong conclusions. Still, her words stung, and he couldn't help thinking they'd been right about keeping their relationship superficial. Their approach to life was so different that they didn't have a hope of ever fully understanding each other.

'That's not the same thing,' Mallika was saying. 'She's got kids and a husband, hasn't she?'

Shirin was in the process of divorcing her husband. That was another thing Darius had never told Mallika, and this was definitely not the right time. Suddenly his plans for a glorious morning with Mallika had turned into an ugly argument and he coulnd't wait for it to be over.

'Mallika—' he said, but she interrupted him.

'I'm sorry,' she said. 'This isn't any of my business, and I'm getting a bit too emotional about it. I miss my own parents and I can't understand you leaving yours behind while you go off to discover yourself, or what-ever. So I'm not being rational, and I've probably said a bunch of things I shouldn't have.'

Her voice was shaking a little, and Darius felt his anger dissipate as quickly as it had flared up.

'It's all right,' he said. 'You're right, in a way. But my family and my decisions don't have anything to do with the situation you and Aryan are in. I really do want to help, Mallika. Don't keep pushing me away.'

'I'm not,' she said. 'It's just…very tough talking about him with anyone. Even you. It feels like I'm betray-ing him. And I love spending time with you, but I feel guilty every minute because I know he needs me more than you do.'

There was a longish pause, after which Darius spoke. 'I can understand that,' he said slowly. 'But what about what *you* need?'

'I don't know, Darius, but I do know that I have to put him first. That's what you do when it comes to family— you don't just go off and leave them to it.'

Family would always be her priority, but as she began to calm down she realised how harsh that must have sounded to Darius. It had been a long and tiring week, and Aryan's moods and ingratitude had pushed her over the edge. A weak, but insistent part of her kept saying that she should apologise and do whatever he wanted, but she squashed it firmly.

Luckily, before she could say anything, he said, 'All right, then. I guess I'll see you around the office next week.'

His voice was remote and expressionless, and Mallika just got to say a brief goodbye before he cut the call.

She put the phone on her bedside table and flopped back into bed to stare at the ceiling. It was all very well to tell herself that she'd get over Darius in a bit—right now she felt as if she'd succeeded in cutting her heart out with a rusty knife. He had been genuinely trying to help her, to connect with her better, and she'd said some unforgivable things to him. No wonder he'd sounded as if he never wanted to see her again.

She tried to focus on Aryan instead. Darius wasn't the first person to say that he needed professional help, though he'd said it far more bluntly than most. Mallika had done her best to shield her younger brother from the aftermath of their parents' death, but he'd actually been there when the accident had happened. He'd escaped completely unharmed, but since then he'd been a shell of his former self.

Mallika and he had been close when they were growing up, but despite her best efforts she hadn't been able to get him to talk to her about what was wrong. And the more she tried to draw him out, the more silent he became.

The only time Aryan seemed really happy was when he was in front of his laptop, staring at the flickering screen as he traded stocks and moved money around from one set of investments to another. He had inherited just the right mix of talents from his father and mother to be a formidable trader, and he had almost doubled the money they had inherited from their parents over the last year.

Aryan lived most of his life online—he worked online and bought everything he needed on various websites and had it delivered to the flat. They had a cook and a cleaner, and of course he had Mallika for anything else. He no longer needed to go out at all.

After a while, she had stopped pushing him to talk, and that had had the result of making him more and more dependent on her. He tried to stick as close to her as he could whenever she was at home, and messaged her constantly when she was at work. Mallika sometimes found herself wishing he'd leave her alone—he was as demanding as he'd been when he was three and had toddled behind her everywhere like a pudgy little shadow.

Mallika sighed as she got out of bed. There were little sounds coming from the kitchen that indicated that Aryan was awake and foraging for breakfast. She'd forgotten to order groceries the day before, and there wasn't any ready stuff that he could eat. She'd need to make him some *upma* or something before she got ready and left to catch the eleven o'clock ferry to Alibagh.

There was a long queue for the ferry at the Gateway of India and Mallika joined it, cradling her bright green tote in her arms. The sun was beating down uncomfortably on her head and she wished she'd thought to wear a hat in addition to the sunglasses that she'd perched on her nose.

The glasses served the dual purpose of saving her eyes from the sun as well as concealing quite how puffy they were. Post-breakfast, with a morose and monosyllabic brother, she'd gone to her room and had a good cry.

It hadn't done much for her looks, but at least she felt a lot calmer than she had in the morning.

'Excuse me, would you mind keeping my place for me in the queue for a few minutes?' the woman in front of her said. 'My son wants an ice cream, and if I don't get it for him right now he'll whine for the entire hour that we're on the ferry.'

'No, I won't,' the pudgy youngster standing next to her said indignantly.

He had a pronounced accent which Mallika couldn't quite place—it wasn't American, but it was close.

'You promised me an ice cream last week and I didn't whine when you didn't buy it, did I?'

'Of course you did,' his slightly older sister chimed in.

Their mother groaned. 'Can it, both of you,' she said. 'Do you want ice cream or not?'

'Want ice cream,' both of them said firmly.

The woman turned back to Mallika. 'Sorry,' she said. 'They're at a terribly argumentative stage. So—is it okay if I leave the queue for a minute?'

'Yes, of course,' Mallika said.

'Of course it's okay if you *leave*,' the girl said scornfully. 'The point is, will she let you back in the line when you come back?'

'I will,' Mallika promised, her lips twitching slightly. The girl was around nine, dignified, knobbly-kneed and totally adorable.

'Thank you so much,' the mother said with evident relief, grabbing her children's hands. 'Come on, people.'

Mallika gazed after her as she walked towards the ice cream vendor, holding a child's hand in each of her own. She had a slight twang to her accent as well, and there was something about her that was vaguely familiar.

The queue had moved quite a bit before the woman came back, breathless and clutching ice cream bars in each hand.

'Oh, thanks,' she said in relief as Mallika waved to her. 'Here—I forgot to ask you which flavour you'd like. So I got chocolate and vanilla both—you take the one you like and I'll have the other.'

'You shouldn't have,' Mallika said, taking the chocolate bar gratefully. 'But thank you so much—it's so hot I feel like I'm about to melt.'

'It'll be more pleasant on the boat,' the woman said. 'Come on, now, kids—be careful on the stairs or you'll slip and fall in the water.'

'Papa would have carried us if he was here,' the boy grumbled.

His sister glared at him. 'Well, he isn't, so *manage*,' she said fiercely. 'Whine-pot.'

'Cry-baby,' the boy retorted. 'Mud-face.'

'Muuuummm...' the girl said.

'Be *nice*, people!' the woman snapped.

'I can carry you, if you like,' Mallika offered. 'Your mum's got too many bags to handle.'

The boy looked as if he wasn't sure which was worse—being carried in public by a *girl*, or having to walk down the stairs on his own. His evident fear of heights won over, and he held his chubby arms up to Mallika.

'I wish Papa was here,' the boy said defiantly once she'd picked him up, and Mallika wondered where their father was.

'He divorced us,' the girl said in a fierce whisper to her brother. 'Stop whining or I'll punch you in the face.'

Their mother sighed. 'So much for being dignified

and discreet,' she said, and gave Mallika an artificially bright smile. 'I'm so sorry you're being subjected to this.' In a whisper, she continued, 'My husband ran away with his secretary a few months ago and we're still trying to deal with it.'

Under the smile she looked tired and defeated, and Mallika's heart went out to her. 'Men can be pigs,' she said quietly once they were all on the ferry. 'I'm sorry— it must be tough for you.'

'I'm thrilled to be rid of the cheating bastard, actually,' the woman replied in an undertone as they climbed to the upper deck behind the kids. 'But it's tough on the kids. If he'd given me a choice I might have actually stayed with him to keep them happy. As it turned out he didn't, so here we are—back in India.'

'Where were you before this?'

'Canada,' she said. 'But I'm happy to be back with my family.' They had reached the upper deck, and the woman looked around. 'Are you in the A/C section as well?' she asked.

Mallika shook her head. 'I prefer the sea breeze,' she said. 'See you in a bit.'

She took a seat towards the front of the ferry, where she didn't have to look at other people, and leaned her head gratefully against the cold guard rail. She'd loved these ferry rides to Alibagh when she was a teenager. Aryan had still been a kid then, and he'd used to run around madly while Mallika stood near the railing, soaking in the sun and the sea breeze.

Even in those days she'd been more of an outdoor person than Aryan was—he'd preferred the lower deck, and after a few arguments their mother had started buying two tickets for the upper deck and two for the lower, so that they didn't fight.

Mallika cast a glance towards the air-conditioned cabin where the woman and her kids had gone. *'I might have actually stayed with him to keep them happy...'* It sounded so terribly sad, when the woman was clearly happier without her husband.

Mallika wondered whether her own mother would have been happier without her father. She'd definitely been more than capable of taking care of herself, but their extended family was extremely conservative. Maybe she'd stayed so that she didn't have to be cut off from them. Or maybe she'd not wanted to separate Aryan and Mallika from their father.

She still felt guilty when she thought of how much trouble they'd given their mother during their growing up years. It had only been when she was in her late teens that Mallika had begun to understand why her mother worked so hard and was so grim and serious most of the time. And even then she'd not known the full story.

As she'd told Darius, her father had lost most of his money in the stock market crash of the eighties—what she hadn't realised for many years was that her mother had been supporting the family ever since. When she'd found out she'd been more sympathetic, but she still hadn't been able to understand why her mother couldn't loosen up a little...be a little more fun.

Her attention was attracted by the girl and her mother coming out of the air-conditioned cabin. The girl's face was distinctly green.

'I'll be all right on my own,' she was telling her harassed mother. 'You go inside and be with Rehaan.'

'I'm not leaving you here on your own,' the mother said. 'Are you still feeling pukey?'

'Not that much,' the girl said, pushing her way through the crowded deck to come and stand next to Mallika by the railing. 'It's better in the breeze.'

'Seasick?' Mallika asked, and the woman nodded.

'The sea's really choppy, and it's a bit disorientating inside the cabin. Rehaan's refusing to come out. I should have just stayed home instead of trying to take these two out for a weekend break.'

'I'll be okay on my own,' the girl insisted.

'I can keep an eye on her, if you like,' Mallika offered.

The woman laughed. 'You know, this is the part I love about being back in India,' she said. 'It feels like being part of one big family. I'm Shirin, by the way, and this is Ava.'

'Pleased to meet you,' Mallika said, grinning back at her. 'So, if you like, you can leave Ava with me and go be with Rehaan.'

'He'll be all right on his own for a bit,' Shirin said, and lowered her voice a little. 'It's Ava I worry about—it's not as safe for a girl as it is for a boy, and I don't know how to explain that to her. And I'd die before I admit it to her, but I'm feeling a bit seasick as well.'

They were both silent for a while, watching Ava as she waved to a flock of seagulls following the ferry.

Ava was too engrossed in the seagulls to hear them, and Mallika said impulsively, 'I don't mean to be intrusive, but you said that you'd have stayed with your husband for the sake of the kids—it's not worth it. You'll be much happier on your own.'

Shirin turned to look at her, raising her brows a little. 'Sounds like you're speaking from personal experience.'

'Sort of,' Mallika admitted.

She'd never spoken about this before, and confiding in a stranger wasn't the kind of thing she normally went in for. Still, there was something about Shirin that made Mallika want to talk to her.

'My dad had affairs,' she said. 'Many of them. My mum put up with them—I guess she didn't have much of a choice—but me and my brother didn't understand why she was unhappy most of the time and we tended to blame her a little. My dad was fun, only he wasn't around much—it was only when I was in my teens that I figured out that he was a pathetic excuse for a husband.'

'No wonder you don't have a high opinion of men,' Shirin said. 'Is your dad still like that?'

'He died in an accident,' Mallika said. 'Along with my mum.'

'Oh, my…' Shirin said sympathetically. 'That sucks.'

Mallika nodded. There was something oddly familiar about Shirin's reaction, but she couldn't put her finger on who she reminded her of.

'Anyway, what I was trying to say is that your kids might be a bit upset now, but it's better for them to be growing up with you.'

'That's good to hear,' Shirin said. 'Most of the time I'm sure I'm doing the right thing, but sometimes I won-der. The kids miss their dad, and they miss Canada, and I'm not really sure how I'm going to manage.'

'Where do you work?' Mallika asked.

'I don't,' Shirin said with a sigh. 'I sponge off my brother. But I'm planning to start once I get the kids settled in school.'

Mallika wondered for an instant what it would be like to have a brother she didn't have to worry about, then shook herself. Aryan might be a bit of a liability, but she wouldn't swap her own life for Shirin's for anything.

'Older brother?' she asked, for the sake of something to say.

'No—younger,' Shirin said. 'I used to make his life hell when he was a kid, but he's—without exaggeration—the best brother a girl could have.'

There was a little pause, and then she went on.

'My parents offered me a place in their flat, but it was impossible to manage. They're old, and set in their ways, and the kids drove them crazy. My brother had a flat in the same building and he's turning it over to me.'

'Has he moved out already?' Mallika asked, though she already knew the answer.

It had taken a while for the penny to drop, but she'd finally realised why Shirin seemed so familiar. She didn't look much like Darius—she was petite and sharp-featured—but some of her mannerisms were just like his, and their smiles were identical.

'Yes, he's rented a hideously expensive place in Parel,' she was saying now. 'He says he's enjoying being on his own, but I still feel terribly guilty. Anyway, he's going overseas in a few months—some complicated "finding himself" kind of journey. I'm happy for him, but I'll miss him like crazy.'

And so will I, Mallika thought to herself, feeling suddenly very shallow and stupid.

It hadn't even occurred to her to ask Darius *why* he'd given his flat to his sister. All this while she'd thought Darius was being callous about Aryan, not realising that he took his responsibilities as a sibling quite as seriously as she did.

'Are your parents okay with your brother going away?'

she asked, the words slipping out before she could help herself.

Shirin nodded. 'He's wanted to do it for as long as I can remember, and he planned his trip a couple of years ago,' she said. 'He's had to cancel it twice already—once because Dad had a heart attack, and a second time because I'd come back to India to have my second baby. Our grandmother fell down and broke pretty much every bone in her hip around the same time, and poor Darius was saddled with looking after all of us *and* paying the medical bills. Luckily he was minting money by then, so the bills weren't a problem, but he went crazy trying to look after everyone at the same time. It doesn't help that we're a bit of an eccentric family too... Anyway, this time hopefully he'll get away before one of us does something stupid.'

Rehaan stuck his head out of the cabin, and Shirin hurried towards him while Mallika tried to get her disordered thoughts back on track. This didn't really change things. If anything, it underlined the fact that she wasn't suited to be with a man like Darius even if he had been ready for a relationship.

Any other woman would have tried to find out about his family—*she* was so hung up about her own that she'd avoided the subject of his completely. From what Shirin had said, Darius was as unlike her father as he could be—he was responsible and trustworthy. And she'd made all kinds of assumptions about him that were totally untrue. Worse, she'd accused him of not caring for his family—and he hadn't even defended himself.

Shirin waved to her as they got off at the jetty, and Mallika saw them get into a car that had the logo of an expensive resort printed on the side. Alibagh had been a sleepy little seaside town during her growing up years, but in the last decade high end hotels and villas had gone up all around the place. Property prices had rocketed as well, and her mother's decision to buy a bungalow there had been more than vindicated.

It took her most of the day to get a contractor to commit on the money and the time it would take him to get the leakage in the Alibagh house fixed. It didn't turn out to be as expensive as she'd feared, but she'd need to make a few more trips to the house over the next few weeks.

She grimaced at the thought. Even now she couldn't bring herself to go into the kitchen and cook a meal for herself, and she ended up sitting in the living room and eating the packed lunch she'd brought with her.

It was ironic, she thought—after all the grief and heartache he'd caused her mother, her father had finally died trying to save her from the fire. If there was an afterlife, perhaps her mother had forgiven him. Mallika still couldn't bring herself to do so.

The weeks after her parents' death would have been horrific enough without having to deal with her father's mistress. She was a virago of a woman, out for all that she could get, and finally Mallika's father's impecuniousness made sense—all this while he'd been supporting her on the side.

Mallika's mother had known, and she'd been careful to make sure that all her investments and the property she'd bought were either in her own name or in her children's. Even so, there had been a bitter battle to hold on to Mallika's grandparents' flat, which her father had inherited, and his mistress had done all she could to claim a share of it. Finally, when she hadn't been able to take any more, Mallika had paid her off—she didn't regret the money, but the experience had left her very bitter.

Once she'd sorted everything out with the contractor and the caretaker, and made advance payments to the workers, Mallika headed back to the jetty. There was just about time for her to catch the last ferry out, and she settled herself into a corner seat with a sigh. She hadn't been able to stop thinking about Darius all day, and impulsively she pulled out her phone and dialled his number.

The phone rang a few times, but Darius didn't pick up and she dropped it back into her bag. Calling him had been a stupid idea anyway—he was probably out partying with his friends.

Feeling suddenly very lost and alone, she shut her eyes and tried not to think about him. The images kept coming, though, and she had to blink very hard to stop tears from welling into her eyes. Damn Darius—he was proving far more difficult to forget about than she'd thought.

CHAPTER EIGHT

IT WAS PAST eleven when Darius finally got back home. He'd gone to the tennis court in his building to see if he could catch a game, and he'd run into an ex-colleague who was now a neighbour. They'd played a couple of gruelling sets, after which they'd walked down to a nearby bar to watch a football match over beer and chicken wings. His ex-colleague was a cheerful, sporty sort of man who didn't go in for deep thinking—he was the perfect companion to take Darius's mind off Mallika.

Once he was back in the flat, though, the morning's conversation replayed itself in his head. He was able to be a little more objective now, and he could see things from Mallika's point of view. She was going through a tough time with Aryan, and she wasn't yet over her parents' death—she couldn't be blamed for not wanting to complicate her life by getting into a relationship with a man who was about to go away for who knew how long.

He'd left his phone in the flat, and picked it up now to see three messages from his sister. Shirin had taken the kids out for a weekend on the beach, and while she said it had got off to a rocky start they seemed to be fine now.

He smiled as he read through her quirky messages

about the kids' reactions to the hotel and the pool—and the last message read: Hired a babysitter and am now off to the spa!!!

He was still smiling as he scrolled through the list of calls he'd missed, and his expression stilled as he saw the call from Mallika. Damn, she'd called over four hours ago—she must have thought he was purposely avoiding talking to her.

He glanced at the time—too late to call her back, but he could text her. They both used the same mobile chat app, and he checked her status. It said she was last on at ten twenty-five p.m., which wasn't that long ago.

Hey—sorry I missed your call, he typed. Had forgotten my phone was at home.

Mallika reached out for her phone as it pinged. She still kept in touch with a few school friends through mobile chat—most of them lived overseas now, and she was used to getting texts at odd hours from them. But this time it wasn't Naina or Kirti messaging about their latest boyfriends…

No worries, she typed. I just wanted to apologise for being so rude when we spoke in the morning.

The reply was almost instantaneous.

I'm sorry too. I shot my mouth off a bit.

Cool, so we're quits.

Mallika thought a bit and added a smiley.

How was Alibagh?

Not bad. I got most of my work done. Guess what—I met your sister on the ferry on the way out.

She took the ferry? I thought she was taking the speed-boat!

Must have changed her mind. She's really nice, by the way. And so are the kids.

She didn't mention meeting you! I saw her messages a minute ago.

We just had a random conversation. I figured out she was your sister from something she said.

You didn't introduce yourself?

No L wasn't sure if she'd know who I was.

I've talked about you. No details, though.

Thank heaven no details.

Mallika typed the words, even though she felt flattered that he'd spoken about her at home.

She's my older sister—what d'you expect?

The text was quickly followed by another.

Can you talk? Texting feels a bit teenagerish...

Teenagers don't type full words. Can't talk L A's a light sleeper and his room's right next to mine.

There was a pause of a couple of minutes, as if Darius was deciding how to respond.

OK, got it.

Will the flamingos still be there tomorrow?

Guess so.

Can we go?

Guess so.

Mallika stared at the phone in frustration. The problem with texting was that she couldn't figure out whether he wanted to see her or not—*Guess so* was as vague as it got. She was about to type a message when his chat window popped up again.

Should I pick you up?

Can meet you there. But no pressure, seriously, if you don't want to go.

Isn't that my line?

It was—this time I'm the one who's asking you to come!

I want to see you. The flamingos are incidental.

They agreed on a time, and Mallika put her phone back on her bedside table, feeling strangely euphoric.

Mallika took a cab to Sewri the next morning. She'd arranged to meet Darius at the path that led to the mudflats, and her body was thrumming with nervous energy—she had to take several deep breaths to calm herself before she got out of the cab.

The cabbie gave her a jaundiced look as she fumbled in her wallet for change. 'Should I wait?' he asked. 'You won't get a cab back from here.'

Mallika shook her head and handed him the fare. 'No, I have a ride back.'

'I can wait anyway,' the man said. 'In case whoever you're meeting doesn't turn up.'

Goodness, she hadn't even thought of that! What if Darius didn't come?

She spotted him as soon as she'd dismissed the thought as ridiculous, and her breath caught in her throat. He looked achingly familiar and wildly desirable at the same time.

'He's here—you don't need to wait,' she muttered to the cabbie, and got out of the cab, standing stock-still as Darius came up to meet her.

He was wearing a dark blue open-necked T-shirt over jeans, and he looked good enough to eat. It took a significant effort of will not to throw her arms around him.

'Hello,' she said shyly—but she didn't get any further. Darius put an arm around her and pulled her against his side in a surprisingly fierce hug.

'Good morning,' he said. 'Come on, let's go.'

There was an ancient shipwreck at the beginning of the mudflats that gave the best view of the flamingos.

There were people milling around, and Darius took his arm away from her shoulders to help her up the rickety ladder.

'I can manage,' Mallika said, but just at that instant her foot slipped a little and she had to cling onto him for support.

'I'm sure you can,' he said soothingly. 'I just feel like holding your hand for a bit.'

Put like that, she could hardly say no, and the ladder *was* rickety…with a thirty-foot drop to the mud below.

The flamingos were amazing—flocks and flocks of them, perched among the mangroves that grew out of the sludgy mud. They were a bright salmon-pink, and they were showing off a little—taking off and swooping back onto their perches in little groups. Some of them were busy looking for food, and a guide nearby was explaining their migratory habits to a bunch of serious-looking kids.

'Did you ever bring Ava and Rehaan here?' Mallika asked, cuddling in a little closer to Darius. Public displays of affection weren't normally her thing, but she could hardly bear to keep her hands off him.

He nodded. 'Last week,' he said. 'I hear Shirin confided in you quite a bit on the ferry yesterday?'

Mallika looked up in surprise. 'Is she back?' she asked. 'I thought they were away for the weekend?'

'She called this morning,' Darius said. 'Thanks for pepping her up. She's going through a bit of a guilt trip, keeping the kids away from their dad.'

'I figured that,' Mallika said slowly.

If Shirin had relayed their conversation to him, she'd probably told him what Mallika had said about her own family.

Feeling suddenly a little vulnerable, she leaned her

head against his arm and said, 'When you told me she'd moved back to India I didn't realise she was going through a divorce.'

'I guess we didn't talk about her much,' he said, even though he'd consciously *not* told her. She had enough problems of her own without him moaning about his family to her as well, and they had agreed not to talk too much about personal family matters.

'I'm sorry about all I said yesterday,' Mallika said. 'I made a lot of assumptions about you that were completely wrong.'

'It doesn't matter,' he said quietly. 'It was as much my fault as yours—it was natural that you jumped to a few wrong conclusions.'

'*Very* wrong conclusions,' she said, her mouth twisting into a wry smile. 'From what Shirin said, you've done far more for your family than I've ever done for mine.'

'And I'm now escaping from them,' he said, holding up a hand when she began to protest. 'It's true,' he said. 'Not exactly the way you thought it was, but it's true all the same. They've come to depend on me a lot over the last few years. My mother says she's fine with me leaving, but I know what she'd really like is for me to marry a nice Parsi girl and settle down in Mumbai for the rest of my life. Shirin would like me to hang around and be a father figure for my niece and nephew. And my father would like me to join his golf club and start taking an interest in fine wines.'

It was the most Mallika had ever heard him say about his family, and it took her a few seconds to absorb it fully. 'It all sounds rather overwhelming,' she admitted.

'It is,' he said. 'I love my family a lot, and if they really needed me I'd cancel my travels for a third time without a single regret. But with Shirin around I think they'll be fine.'

'I'm sure they will,' Mallika said, wanting more than anything to remove the slight uncertainty lurking in his eyes. 'You should go—especially since it's something you've wanted to do for so long.'

'It's bigger than me, in a way,' he said, and laughed slightly. 'This whole need to go out and see the world. Shirin says it's inherited—some ancient Persian wanderlust gene that's skipped a few generations.'

'Maybe she's right,' Mallika said, reaching out to take his hand.

There was a tinge of sadness in her voice as she thought of how different the two of them were. His family sounded like the kind she'd always longed for and, while she understood his motivations a lot better now, she knew that she wouldn't have taken the same decisions in his place. She craved stability and was comfortable with the conservative values of a traditional family, whereas Darius wanted to break out, challenge himself and push boundaries.

He helped her down the ladder, and once they were on dry land again turned her to face him.

'Want to come over?' he asked, and she nodded, her throat suddenly dry.

There was no mistaking his meaning—and there was also no point bringing up the rules again. Their attraction was too strong to fight, and the most she could hope for was that it would die away after a while without doing too much damage.

Neither of them spoke during the short drive to his flat, their heightened anticipation too intense to allow for casual conversation. Mallika found that her knees were trembling just a bit as Darius unlocked the flat and let her in.

She had barely stepped inside when he bolted the door and turned to take her into his arms.

'Welcome back,' he murmured against her mouth, and then there was no room to talk any more as a tide of pure unadulterated desire overtook both of them.

'What next?' Darius asked many hours later. 'I guess a few of the rules just went out of the window.'

'I guess,' she said, trailing her hand slowly down his chest.

She didn't want to think about practical stuff right now, and Darius's question had brought her back to reality with a bump.

'We can take each day as it comes, can't we?' she asked. 'I mean, some of those rules I made were downright silly.'

'I agree,' Darius said, and it sounded so heartfelt that both of them burst out laughing.

Mallika pressed herself closer to him. With her slim, pliant body and sparkling, naughty eyes, Mallika was almost impossible to resist, and Darius bent his head to capture her lips under his.

'You know, Shirin really liked you,' he said.

'I liked her too,' Mallika said, feeling absurdly flattered.

Darius reached out and tucked a stray strand of hair behind her ear.

'I think it's time for you to meet the family,' he said musingly.

Mallika looked up in alarm. 'Whose family?' she asked.

'The Prime Minister's,' Darius said. 'Whose do you think? Mine.'

'I thought we'd agreed not to tell them!' Mallika said.

'We did. You're going to be my scary colleague-cum-landlady. Shirin's guessed, but to my parents you'll be just one more among my many admirers. Come on, I'd like you to meet them—they're a little crazy, but they're fun.'

Mallika couldn't bring herself to say no—she still didn't know *why* Darius would want to take her home, though.

'Aunt Freny's going to be there as well,' he told her. 'You'll like her.'

'What should I wear?' she asked.

'I've no idea,' Darius said. 'We'll be going from work, so regular office gear should be fine. My parents aren't particular.'

Particular or not, Mallika felt devoutly grateful that she'd dressed up a little when she met Darius's perfectly groomed mother the next day. All of five feet tall, she was like a Dresden figurine with her pink cheeks and carefully styled snow-white hair. She gave Mallika a polite kiss on the cheek, her flowery perfume enveloping them as she ushered Mallika and Darius into the room.

'Papa Mistry, this is Darius's landlady,' she announced, and Darius's father peered short-sightedly at her.

'She looks too young and too pretty to be a landlady,' he said firmly. '*Now* I know why Darius didn't want to live here any more.'

'He didn't want to live here because this place is like

a mausoleum,' Aunt Freny grumbled. 'Or a madhouse when those kids of Shirin's turn up. Little devils.'

'Don't you dare call my grandchildren names,' Mrs Mistry said, her eyes narrowing dangerously. 'They're perfectly angelic if you know how to handle them.'

'With a pair of long-handled tongs,' Aunt Freny muttered.

Mrs Mistry pretended not to hear her. 'Do sit down, child,' she said to Mallika. 'How do you take your tea? One cube of sugar? And milk?'

The tea tray had a tea cosy on it with a fat little teapot inside, and a tiny jug of milk with a bowl full of sugar cubes next to it. Mallika looked curiously at Mrs Mistry as she poured the tea. She'd seen tea served so elaborately only in British period movies on TV—real, live people drinking it this way was a novelty. Her own mother had always just boiled everything together and then strained it into cups.

'So you met Darius at work?' Mr Mistry asked, leaning forward curiously. 'This is the first time he's brought a girl home.'

'The first time this month,' Aunt Freny said promptly, and Mallika dissolved into laughter.

Aunt Freny was adorable—Mallika's own relatives tended towards the stiff and formal, and she wished she'd had someone like Aunt Freny around when she was going up.

'Freny is our *enfant terrible*,' Mr Mistry said indulgently. 'Tell us about what you do, Mallika. Darius said you work in real estate investments? How did you end up there?'

He seemed genuinely interested, and he knew far more about real estate than most people did.

Shirin trooped in with her children when they were halfway through the conversation, and Rehaan promptly clambered onto his grandfather's lap.

'Where's Great-Granny?' he demanded.

Mr Mistry turned to his wife. 'Is Mummy still asleep?' he enquired.

'No, I'll go and call her,' Mrs Mistry said, and a few minutes later a tiny, very frail-looking old lady emerged from somewhere inside the house.

Darius got up to help her to a chair. 'Meet my grandmother,' he said to Mallika. 'She was an army nurse during the Second World War.'

The elder Mrs Mistry was alert and very garrulous. But with the children running around, and Shirin keeping up a parallel conversation on school admissions, poor Mallika could hardly understand what she was saying, and after a while she gave Darius an appealing look.

'Darius, you should take Mallika out dancing instead of making her sit with us old folks,' Aunt Freny said.

'I used to love dancing when I was a girl,' Darius's grandmother said wistfully. 'My Rustom used to waltz so well.'

'He used to step on everyone's toes,' the irrepressible Aunt Freny said. 'And sometimes he got the steps wrong. But he looked good—I'll give you that.'

'Darius, I'm coming to your building on Saturday,' Ava announced. 'To swim in the pool.'

'You're very welcome,' Darius said. 'I won't be there, but don't let that stop you.'

'Why can't you swim in the club, *dikra*?' Mrs Mistry asked, shooting a quelling look at Darius.

'Because the club pool is full of old hairy men,' Ava said. 'Can I just say—*ewwwww*?'

'Men *should* be hairy,' Mrs Mistry said. 'Not too much, but all these models and actors nowadays with waxed chests—they look terrible. What do you think, Mallika?'

Completely thrown by the sudden appeal for her opinion, Mallika floundered. 'I...uh...I guess it's fashionable nowadays.'

'Darius doesn't wax his chest,' Rehaan volunteered. 'I saw him in the pool last week and he's got hair. Not the orang-utan kind—just normal.'

'Thank you, Rehaan,' Darius said, getting to his feet. 'And on that note I think we should leave. People who aren't used to our family can handle us only in small doses.'

'If you mean Mallika, I think she's made of sterner stuff,' Shirin said, giving Mallika a friendly smile.

'Do you like orchids?' Aunt Freny asked abruptly.

Mallika nodded, and Freny reached behind her chair and produced a flowering orchid in a small ceramic pot.

'This is for you,' she said, handing it to Mallika with a firm little nod. 'Don't overwater it, and make sure it's not in the sun.'

Mallika took the orchid, and as Darius looked all set to leave she stood up as well, and followed him to the door.

'It was really nice meeting all of you,' she said, giving the four generations in the room a comprehensive sort of smile.

'It was lovely meeting you too, *dikra*,' Mrs Mistry said warmly. 'Darius, you must bring her again.'

'Yes, sure,' he said drily, but he was smiling as he bent down to kiss his mother.

He waited till they were in the car before turning to her and raising his eyebrows.

'Well? Did they scare you?'

She laughed and shook her head. 'They were fun,' she said.

And so they were—but she wasn't sure why Darius had decided that it was the right time to introduce her to his family. After all, he was going away, so what they had couldn't go anywhere.

Back at Darius's flat, she shut the front door behind her and leaned against it, her eyes dancing as she looked at him.

'I need to refresh my memory,' she said. 'Exactly *how* hairy is that chest of yours?'

CHAPTER NINE

'ONE OF MY schoolfriends is coming from the US this Friday,' Darius said a few days later. 'We haven't met in years, so I've invited him to stay with me over the weekend. Shirin and a few other people are coming over for dinner on Saturday. Would you like to come?'

Mallika hesitated. She'd insisted that Darius still did not tell his parents the truth about them, the way she'd not told Aryan or any of *her* relatives, but Shirin had guessed anyway—and meeting a few people for dinner trumped not seeing Darius at all for the entire weekend.

'Okay,' she said. 'D'you need help planning the dinner?'

'No, I'll outsource everything,' he said. 'There's a friend of mine who does catering for Parsi weddings. I'll just ask her to manage it.'

'Catering… Exactly how many people are you inviting?'

'Around twenty-five or so, I thought,' Darius said, not noticing Mallika's horrified expression. 'The living room's big enough to hold that many, and if it isn't they can go and stand on the balcony.'

The intercom rang and he went to answer it, leaving Mallika to deal with her panicky reaction to meeting twenty-five of Darius's friends all at once. She always felt shy in large groups—while not agoraphobic, like Aryan, she still preferred meeting a maximum of three or four people at a time.

Darius came back after a short conversation—presumably with the security guard who screened visitors at the main gate.

'I bought a painting last week and it's on its way upstairs now,' he said. 'I was hoping I'd get a chance to show it to you before I left for Delhi again.'

Nidas had recently taken over a smaller firm, and Darius was travelling to Delhi almost every week to manage the merger of the two companies' assets. It was stressful, and Mallika knew he didn't enjoy the trips. She hoped it was because they took him away from her and the small amount of time they had left together...

'I didn't realise you had to go this week as well,' she said. 'When's the takeover going to be complete?'

'At least another two months,' Darius said, sighing as he pulled her close. 'It's crazy. There's so much to do. But it's a big acquisition for Nidas, and in the long term it will make a big difference to our share value. It's just a difficult process right now—especially since the need for greater efficiencies means some of their staff are being let go.'

He was silent for a while, and Mallika hugged him back without saying anything either. It was the first time he had touched her seeking comfort, she realised—so far everything had been about sex. In a way she felt closer to him this way than when they were making love, and it was an odd sensation.

The doorbell rang, and he let her go to open the door.

The painting was carefully packaged in layers of bubble wrap, and Darius had to use a knife to get it out.

'What d'you think?' he asked as he knelt to prop the painting against the nearest wall.

The painting had appealed to him the minute he'd seen it, tucked away in the corner of a little art gallery he patronised. A mass of swirling colours, it managed to capture exactly the feel of an Indian market—you could almost smell the spices and feel the dust and the heat.

Mallika looked at the signature at the bottom right-hand corner. 'This is a good example of the artist's work,' she said, sounding impressed. 'It would have been a brilliant investment if you'd bought it a few years ago.'

'I bought it because I like it,' Darius said, a puzzled look on his face. 'It isn't an *investment*.'

'That's a good reason as well,' Mallika said, sounding amused. 'I'm sorry—I guess I've been working on investments too long to remember that people sometimes buy expensive things just because they like them.'

'Different perspectives,' he said, laughing as he got back to his feet.

He came closer and slid his hands around her waist, making her shiver with longing.

'Stay for dinner?' he asked, nuzzling the most sensitive part of her neck.

'I can't,' she said regretfully. 'I need to get back home.'

'Stay this once,' he said, pulling her closer, and they kissed once more—a long, drugging kiss that left her with trembling knees and a blind desire to tug his clothes off and spend the rest of the day making love on the living room floor.

'Aryan...' she said.

Darius groaned. 'He'll be okay just this once,' he said. 'We've never spent a night together, Mallika, and I'm leaving soon—we mightn't get another chance.'

Put like that, she found it almost impossible to say no, and after another half-hearted protest she messaged Aryan to let him know that she was staying over at a friend's home.

It was around four in the morning when Mallika woke up with a start. She didn't know what exactly had woken her, but her pulse was pounding as if she'd just finished a gruelling race. Next to her, Darius muttered something in his sleep and put a heavy arm around her, pulling her close to his magnificent chest.

Gingerly, Mallika stretched a hand out to the bedside table to pick up her phone. Perhaps the message tone had woken her—she wouldn't put it past Aryan to be messaging her to come home quickly, or perhaps to pick up some exotic computer accessory on her way home.

The screen was blank, however, and there were no messages at all other than one from her bank offering her 'never before' rates on a loan. Puzzled, she checked the signal—it was at full strength, so that meant Aryan hadn't messaged her at all.

'Darius,' she whispered, and he woke up, blinking a little as the light from the mobile phone display hit his eyes.

'Something wrong?' he asked, sitting up as he took in her expression.

'There's not a single message from Aryan,' she said weakly, realising how stupid she sounded as soon as the words were out of her mouth.

Thankfully, Darius immediately understood what she was trying to say.

'Have you tried calling him?'

'He might be asleep,' she said, and to his eternal credit Darius reached across and put his arms around her.

'Do you want me to take you home?' he asked softly, and she nodded.

There were very few cars on the road, and it took less than ten minutes to drive to her flat. The watchman was asleep, and the lift had been switched off, so they had to climb the stairs to her flat. Mallika's knees were trembling by the time she got to the right floor and un-locked the door.

'Should I wait outside?' Darius asked.

She shook her head. 'Stay in the living room,' she said. 'I'll just check on Aryan—hopefully he's fine and I've dragged you all this way for nothing.'

But he wasn't fine.

When Mallika tiptoed into his room she found him lying stock-still in bed, his eyes wide open and fever-ish. For a few seconds he didn't seem to recognise her, and she sagged onto her knees in relief when he blinked and said, 'Mally...'

'Are you okay?' she asked.

He shook his head. 'I have a headache,' he offered.

She reached out to touch his brow. 'You're burning up,' she said, trying to keep the worry out of her voice. 'I'll get you a paracetamol...maybe you'll feel better after that, okay? Why didn't you call me?'

'I fell in the bathroom and hit my head. I'm not sure where my phone is.'

Mallika clicked on the light—sure enough, there was a huge purpling bruise on his forehead.

'Is he all right?' Darius asked softly as she came out.

She shook her head. 'I don't think he's eaten a single meal since yesterday,' she said. 'And he's got a raging fever. He's also fallen down and hurt his head.'

'I'm so sorry,' he said quietly. 'I shouldn't have pushed you to stay. Is there anything I can do?'

She shook her head angrily. 'It's not your fault,' she said, almost to herself. 'It's mine—for even imagining that I could have a life of my own. Will you get me some biscuits from the kitchen, Darius? I need to make sure he eats something before I give him a paracetamol.'

He nodded, and she went to the medicine cabinet to try and locate the pills. There were only three left in the blister pack, and she popped one out. Darius came back with the biscuits and a glass of water, and she carried them into Aryan's room.

'Eat these first, and then swallow the medicine with the water,' she said.

'I'm not hungry,' Aryan whispered.

Suddenly her control snapped. 'I don't *care*!' she said. 'I stay away for one night and you don't even take care of yourself! Sit up right now and eat—if you don't want me to call an ambulance and get you put in hospital.'

It was the first time she'd ever shouted at him and Aryan sat up in shock, blinking woozily as he took the biscuits from her. Mallika felt horribly guilty, but at least he ate them silently before swallowing the medicine.

'Try and sleep now,' she said, tucking him back into bed. 'I'll call Dr Shetty as soon as it's morning.'

'Stay with me,' Aryan mumbled, reaching for her hand as she got up, but she pulled away.

'I'll be back in a minute,' she said, and went out to Darius.

'I'm so sorry I dragged you out like this,' she said wearily. 'I should have just come home last night.'

'Do you need me to go and fetch a doctor?' he asked.

She shook her head. 'I'll call our family doctor in the morning,' she said. 'I think he'll be okay till then.'

'Right,' Darius said. 'I'll see you when I'm back from Delhi, then—okay?'

She nodded, and he dropped a quick kiss on her forehead before letting himself out.

'He's got an infection. His immunity levels have dropped, staying indoors like this,' the doctor said as he prescribed a course of antibiotics over the phone. 'I'll try to come and see him in a couple of hours, but if he doesn't start leading a normal life this is going to happen more and more often.'

'How's he catching an infection, then, if he isn't going out?'

'From *you*,' he said. 'You work, don't you? *You're* carrying the infections home, but because your immunity levels are normal you're not catching them yourself.'

She spent the next two days nursing Aryan. The doctor visited him, as he'd promised—he'd known both Mallika and Aryan since they were children, and he was as worried about him as Mallika was.

Aryan didn't react as the doctor spoke to him—he'd slipped back into silent mode, and he stared passively at the ceiling while the doctor tried to explain the harm he was doing himself by his self-imposed house arrest.

'The quicker you get him to a good psychiatrist, the better,' Dr Shetty told Mallika when she took him aside to ask what she should do. 'I can treat his physical symptoms, but I can't do much about his mental state. And you're just making it worse by humouring him.'

Perhaps he was right, Mallika thought wearily as she went back inside to persuade her brother to eat something and take his medicine. Perhaps she *was* making her brother worse. Only there was little she could do if he refused to see a psychiatrist—it had been difficult enough persuading him to see Dr Shetty.

She tried to get a psychiatrist to come and meet Aryan, perhaps by pretending to be a friend of hers, but that wasn't the way they operated, apparently. Or at least the reputable ones didn't, and she didn't want to trust Aryan to a quack.

'I mightn't be able to come for dinner on Saturday,' she told Darius when he called one evening.

'Won't Aryan be okay by then?'

'He's over the worst, but he's still a little weak—and he's still not eating properly.'

'Can't one of your relatives stay with him? That aunt of yours who lives nearby?'

'He doesn't want anyone else around,' Mallika said. 'I'm so sorry, Darius.' She was very tired, and her voice shook a little.

Darius immediately softened.

'I'm sorry too,' he said gently. 'Take care. I'll be back from Delhi tonight, and I'll come across and see you on Sunday.'

Mallika was too exhausted to tell him not to come—anyway, Aryan had probably figured out by now that she was dating him. And she wanted to see Darius badly. He'd become the one sane, stable thing in her world, and she knew she was growing horribly dependent on him.

'Are you going out?' Aryan asked on Sunday morning.

It was obvious why he'd asked—Mallika had changed the ancient T-shirt and tracks she normally wore at home for a peasant blouse and Capri pants, and she'd brushed her hair into some semblance of order.

'No,' Mallika said shortly. 'A friend's coming over, and I don't want to look like something from a refugee camp.'

'Is it that Parsi friend of yours? Cyrus, or something?'

'Darius,' she said.

Aryan didn't reply, and she felt a surge of annoyance sweep over her. She'd spent the last few days waiting on him hand and foot—he hadn't bothered to thank her, even once, and now he was behaving as if she didn't have the right to invite a friend over.

Hot words bubbled up to her lips, and she was about to say something when Aryan spoke again.

'Your hair looks just like Mum's when you tie it back like that,' he said, and suddenly Mallika felt tears start to her eyes.

She'd inherited her riotously curly hair from their mother, but while her mum had always carefully brushed her curls into a tight bun, she'd always kept hers short.

Darius gave her a brief kiss, full on the mouth, as he strode into the flat. 'For you,' he said, handing her a box of expensive-looking chocolates. 'How's Aryan doing?'

'He's much better,' she said, taking the chocolates from him. 'Thank you so much.'

He grinned at her. 'You don't need to be so formal,' he said. 'We missed you yesterday—especially Shirin. She's been dying to meet you again.'

'I wish I could have come,' Mallika said regretfully. 'I couldn't leave Aryan alone, though.'

'I'd have been all right on my own,' Aryan said petulantly, walking into the room, his eyes hostile as he looked at Darius. 'Hello,' he said, nodding briefly at him before sitting down on the sofa.

'She was worried about you,' Darius said as he settled his tall frame into the chair opposite Aryan. 'You were quite ill, weren't you?'

The boy looked a little thinner than the last time Darius had seen him, but otherwise he seemed perfectly healthy. And more than capable of looking after himself for one evening.

'I'm better now,' he said, his eyes dark and resentful. 'I can manage on my own if I have to. Anyway, she's hardly at home—whenever she can, she goes away without telling me where she's going.'

The unfairness of it took Mallika's breath away, and she could only stare at Aryan speechlessly.

Darius took one look at her, and took over the conversation. 'I think your sister stays with you for as much time as she can,' he said. 'She can't work from home *every* day, can she?'

Aryan bit his lip, but didn't reply.

Mallika jumped in to dispel the suddenly awkward silence. 'Which would you prefer? Tea or coffee?'

'Tea's good, thanks,' Darius said, and she got up to make it.

'Aryan...?'

'You should know by now that I don't drink the stuff,' he muttered.

Darius frowned.

'Did you have an argument with your sister?' he asked quietly once Mallika had left the room.

Aryan said nothing, but his eyes widened a fraction.

Darius leaned forward. 'I don't think that's the way you normally speak to her,' he said. 'She's completely devoted to you, and she wouldn't be if you were that rude all the time.'

For a second it looked as if Aryan would burst into speech, but then he got to his feet and left the room without a word. A door shut somewhere inside the house, and Darius assumed that he'd gone back to his room. He exhaled slowly, standing up and running a hand through his hair. He very rarely lost his temper, and the sudden surge of anger he'd felt had surprised him as much as it had upset Aryan.

He made his way to the kitchen, where Mallika was pouring tea into two delicate china cups. She looked up at him and smiled, and he felt immediately guilty.

'Sorry—did Aryan leave you alone?' she asked. 'His social skills are a bit basic.'

'I think I sent him away,' he admitted, leaning against the doorway. 'I didn't like the way he spoke to you and I called him out on it. It's not the kind of thing I normally do, but he got under my skin.'

He'd expected Mallika to be annoyed, but she just handed him his teacup, her brow furrowed in thought.

'What did you say to him?' she asked.

He told her, and she shrugged.

'That's pretty mild,' she said. 'Our family doctor spoke to him for a good fifteen minutes yesterday—I'm not sure Aryan even registered what he was saying.'

'How long are you going to manage like this?' Darius asked softly, his hand going out to caress her cheek. 'You need to have a proper life of your own—it just isn't fair to you.'

Mallika went into his arms, burying her face in his

chest. 'I don't know,' she said. 'I need to sit down and have a proper talk with Aryan—maybe I'm reading him all wrong, hovering over him when he could do with some space.'

'It's worth a try,' Darius said, bending down and brushing his lips lightly against hers, making her quiver with need. 'Will you be able to get away for a while in the afternoon? Varun really wanted to meet you.'

For a few seconds Mallika couldn't remember who Varun was. Then she realised he meant the schoolfriend who'd come over from the US.

'At your place?' she asked.

'Yes,' Darius said. 'I'm going down to his hotel to collect him—I'll see you in a couple of hours, okay?'

After Darius left, Mallika went and knocked tentatively on Aryan's door. There was no reply, and she knocked once more before pushing the door open. Aryan was in bed, his face turned towards the wall, and she went in and sat next to him.

'Are you feeling okay?' she asked, putting a gentle hand on his shoulder.

He flipped over onto his back—an abrupt movement that threw her hand off.

'Are you going to marry that guy?' he demanded.

Mallika took a deep breath. Clearly she'd been wrong about the conversation with Darius having had no effect on her brother.

'He's just a friend, Aryan,' she said. 'I'm not planning to get married for a long, long while. Perhaps never.'

Aryan stared at her, his eyes stormy. 'Because of me?' he asked.

She shook her head. She couldn't lay all the blame

at his door, however much she wanted to. 'Because I think I'd make a rotten wife,' she said, a little sadly. 'Don't worry about it, Aryan. Concentrate on getting better. Once you're back on your feet, maybe we could try going out together. Maybe for a walk to Hanging Gardens. Remember how much you used to love going there as a kid?'

'I don't want to go out,' he said, sounding like a truculent kid. 'You don't need to fuss over me, Mally. I'll go when I want to.'

'When will that be? You heard what the doctor said. You're making yourself ill like this.'

'I don't care,' he said, turning away from her again. 'And if I do get ill you can leave me here and go wherever you want. I'm not forcing you to hang around and look after me.'

'You're not,' Mallika said calmly. 'I feel like looking after you because you're my brother and I love you, even though you're perfectly obnoxious at times.'

Aryan didn't react, but when she got up to go he stretched out a hand and held her back without turning around.

Mallika sat down again, reaching across to smooth his hair off his brow.

'I do too,' he muttered under his breath.

She leaned closer. 'You do too, what?' she asked.

'I love you too,' he said, the words so indistinct that she had to strain to hear them. 'And I'm sorry if I'm obnoxious. It's just so hard without Mom.'

His breath hitched in his throat, and Mallika's heart went out to him. They had never been a very demonstrative family, and this was probably the first time she'd told her brother that she loved him since they'd both reached adulthood. Maybe that was part of the reason he was this way—he'd been only twenty-two when their parents had died, and it had to have been tougher on him than her.

'I miss her too,' she said softly.

Aryan said something under his breath that she couldn't hear at all.

'What was that, *baba*?' she asked.

He said in a whisper, 'It was my fault.'

'What was your fault?'

'The accident,' he said. 'I smelt the gas leak when I went into the kitchen to fetch some water. But I forgot about it and I didn't tell Mom.'

'You *knew* about the leak?' Mallika said blankly.

This had never occurred to her. She'd berated herself so many times for not having gone down to Alibagh with the rest of the family—if she'd been around she'd have gone into the kitchen with her mother and smelled the leak. The only reason her mother hadn't noticed was because she'd had a bad head cold and had completely lost her sense of smell. Her father, of course, never stepped into the kitchen, and normally neither did Aryan.

'I've been wanting to tell you ever since,' he said. 'I can't stop thinking about it.'

'Why didn't you tell me?' she demanded, but deep, dry sobs were racking his body now and he couldn't answer.

Mallika got up from the bed, too worked up to stay still. The last two years had been hellish. She still wasn't over the shock and grief of losing both parents together. Almost every day she wished she could have done something to make her mother's life easier—if she'd known about her father's unfaithfulness she'd at least have been more understanding with her mum. Every teenage tantrum she'd thrown had come back to haunt her, and every time she'd taken her father's side in an argument now seemed like a betrayal of her mother.

She looked at Aryan, huddled up on the bed. Aryan had always been petted and spoilt. Her mother had expected Mallika to grow up fast and shoulder responsibilities as soon as she could, but she'd been far more indulgent with Aryan. Her father had been equally indulgent with both, but it had been quite evident that he had valued his son over his daughter.

'Did you tell Dad about the leak?' she asked suddenly, but Aryan was already shaking his head.

'I didn't realise it was serious,' he said in a flat little voice. 'It was only when I heard her screaming... And by then it was too late to do anything.'

He'd been in the garden, Mallika remembered, studying for his college exams. She'd always felt terrible for him—actually being there and unable to help. A lot of her subsequent indulgence towards him had been because she'd thought he was dealing with the trauma still.

'I'm sorry,' Aryan said, his eyes pleading with her. 'I'd do anything to undo what happened...but I can't.'

'I know,' Mallika said. 'I know. I just wish...'

There were so many things she wished—that Aryan had raised the alarm, that he'd at least told their father... The accident hadn't been his fault, but the fact that he could have prevented it made it seem even more tragic than it had before.

Aryan bit his lip, tears welling in his eyes, and Mallika suddenly remembered him as a child, toddling around the kitchen one day and getting underfoot until her mother had picked him up and sat him on the kitchen counter. Mallika had protested at the unfair treatment—*she* never got to sit there—but her mother had laughed and picked her up as well, dancing around the kitchen with her to the tune of an old Bollywood song playing on the radio while Aryan laughed and clapped his hands.

It was one of the very few memories of her childhood she had where her mum was happy and smiling.

'Mum wouldn't have wanted you to torture yourself like this,' she said, going to Aryan. 'It was an accident, and we can't undo any of it. Come here.'

She held out her arms and Aryan crawled into them, hugging her back surprisingly fiercely.

'I'll try to be less of a pain from now on,' he said. 'I wish I'd told you earlier…but, Mally—you don't know how difficult it's been.'

'I can imagine,' she said. 'But it's behind us now. Let's try and get you sorted out.'

For the first time Aryan seemed amenable to the thought of getting help, and Mallika used the opportunity as best as she could. After an hour of coaxing and cajoling she'd managed to get him to agree to going with her to a psychiatrist, and she heaved a sigh of relief. Hopefully things would take a turn for the better now that she knew exactly what was bothering Aryan.

It was only when she went to fetch her phone to make an appointment that she noticed all the messages and missed calls from Darius. Her mouth dropped open in dismay—it was past six, and she'd agreed to meet him and Varun at four.

Fingers trembling a little, she dialled his number.

'I'm so sorry—' she said when he picked up.

'It's all right, Mallika, you don't need to apologise,' he said, sounding resigned. 'Is Aryan okay?'

'Yes,' she said. 'I should have called. I'll explain when we meet, but I really couldn't have come.'

'I understand,' he said. 'I'll see you around at work tomorrow, then.'

Darius was frowning as he put the phone down, and Varun raised his eyebrows. 'You've got it bad, haven't you?' he said.

Darius smiled reluctantly. 'Is it that obvious?'

'Pretty obvious,' Varun said lightly. There was a brief pause, and then Varun said, 'So what are you going to do about it?'

Darius shrugged. 'Nothing,' he said. 'I'm out of here in a few weeks, and I don't know when I'll be back. There's no point trying to do anything about it. In any case, she isn't interested in anything serious either.'

'You could be wrong about that,' Varun murmured.

Darius shook his head. 'I'm not,' he said, but he wondered if it was true.

There were times when he'd thought Mallika was close to admitting that she cared for him, but something seemed to hold her back. Perhaps the same thing that held him back—the realisation that they wanted very different things from life. He was going away, and for Mallika Aryan would always be her first priority.

'If you really care about her there's always a way,' Varun said.

Darius laughed. 'You sound like a soppy women's magazine,' he said lightly, trying not to show how much the words had affected him.

He *did* care about Mallika—in fact, there was a real

risk of his being completely besotted by her. But he couldn't give up his adventures—not when he was finally free to go.

Maybe there *was* a way, and all he had to do was convince her that it would work.

CHAPTER TEN

'I'M SORRY ABOUT YESTERDAY,' Mallika said guiltily. 'Aryan was very upset, and I completely lost track of the time.'

'Don't worry about it,' he said. 'I understand. Is Aryan okay now?'

'Yes,' she said, and before she knew it she was telling him what had happened. 'I think he'll be better now,' she said. 'The guilt was eating him up, and he hadn't told anyone.'

'Poor chap.' Darius's expression was sympathetic. 'That's one hell of a burden to be carrying around. But you're right—if he's talking about it, it's a turn for the better.'

'Let's see how it goes,' Mallika said.

She was being careful not to sound too optimistic, but it was clear to Darius that she was much happier than she'd been in weeks.

'In any case, I'm feeling a lot better about leaving him on his own now. There was a time when I was scared he'd actually harm himself…he was behaving so oddly. Anyway, let's not talk about Aryan—how was your weekend with Varun? Did you guys have a good time?'

'The best,' Darius said, thinking back to his last conversation with Varun. This was probably a good time to bring it up with Mallika, only he wasn't sure how to begin.

'You look very serious,' Mallika said teasingly. 'What are you thinking about so deeply?'

'Not thinking, really. Just…wondering.' He'd meant to lead up to the subject slowly, but his naturally forthright nature made it difficult.

'Wondering about what,' she asked. 'Global warming? Cloud computing? How to save the euro?'

He grinned in spite of himself—Mallika was so often serious that she was irresistible in a lighter mood.

'Nothing quite so earth-shattering,' he said. 'I was thinking about us.'

Her smile faltered a little, and she said, 'Oh…' before making a quick recovery. 'Serious stuff?'

'Well, kind of.' He reached across and took her hands in his. 'Mallika, I know you've had a lot to deal with since your parents died, and I don't want to put you under pressure. But I was thinking—perhaps we don't necessarily need to split up when I leave.'

'Not split up?' she repeated stupidly.

He leaned forward, his expression serious and intense. 'Come with me,' he said. 'If not for the whole trip, at least for part of it.'

Mallika stared at him as if he had suddenly gone crazy. 'What about my job?' she said. 'Aryan?'

'We'll work that out,' he said. 'You can take some time off—I'll square it with Venkat. And Aryan will be fine for a while—especially since it sounds like he might be on the mend now. I'm not asking you to come immediately, if that doesn't work for you. Take some time to settle him properly…maybe ask a relative to be with him. But you need to get away perhaps even more than I do.'

It was an incredibly tempting thought. Being alone with Darius, far away from the problems and complications of her day-to-day life.

Darius meant a lot to her, and if she'd been a little less cynical about life and relationships she'd have fancied herself in love with him. He was committed and caring, and so incredibly hot that she could hardly keep her hands off him. Any other woman would have kidnapped him by now and forced him to marry her—she must be certifiably insane to let the thought of splitting up even cross her mind.

He was still looking at her, the appeal in his eyes almost irresistible, but she slowly shook her head.

'I don't think it would work,' she said slowly. 'I'm not saying I don't want to, but it just makes more sense to end this before it gets too complicated.'

'Mallika…' He took a deep breath. 'How d'you *really* feel about me?'

'I like you,' she said, stumbling over the words a little. 'You make me laugh when I want to cry. You're honest and straightforward, and I can trust you with every secret I have. When you look at me I feel like I'm the most beautiful girl in the world—you're probably the best thing that ever happened to me.'

'I can sense a *but*,' he said softly, though he gripped her hands a little harder.

'But I'm not sure I'm the best thing that ever happened to *you*,' she said in a rush. 'I'm not good for you, Darius. We shouldn't drag this out.'

'And what made you arrive at that conclusion?' he asked.

'We're completely different,' she said. 'You're a straight-forward guy—everything's simple for you—you know exactly what you want. If you feel like doing something, you go ahead and do it. If you like someone, you tell them. If you don't understand what they want, you ask. Things are a lot more complicated for me. Especially when it comes to love and relationships. My parents had the most messed-up marriage ever, and the thought of anything serious or long-term makes me want to run.'

It was probably the most direct conversation they'd ever had, but Darius was beginning to have a bad feeling about the way it was going.

'So we're different?' he said. 'That doesn't mean it can't work. And we're not in the same situation as your parents—we're not even planning to get married.'

Mallika sighed. 'I know,' she said. 'But it isn't just about us being different, or about my parents, Darius. Aryan's better, but I don't think I can leave him for a long while. And I'm not sure if I believe in long-distance relationships. It'll be torture for me, and it might end up being a drag on you. What if you meet someone else? For that matter, what if *I* meet someone else when you're away?'

Darius took a deep breath. 'I'm just saying that we have a good thing going and we don't have to split up when I leave. If either of us meets someone we like better, we can deal with it when it happens.'

'It won't work,' she said unhappily. 'It might be years before you come back—what's the point of trying to drag things out? We'll just make each other unhappy, and when we do split up we'll hate each other. I don't think I could bear that.'

Darius took her by the shoulders and turned her to face him.

'Mallika, do you know how many reasons you've given for not coming with me?'

Mallika shook her head.

'Five,' he said. 'Or maybe six—I lost count after a while. Sweetheart, no one needs five reasons not to do something. One or two are usually enough. Maybe you're overthinking this? For once you should just go with what your heart tells you.'

'I stopped listening to my heart years ago,' she said wryly.

She hadn't been making up the reasons—they were all there, buzzing around like angry bees in her head, and the more she thought about them, the more confused she got.

'Okay, so let's do something less drastic,' Darius said.

He was still holding her by the shoulders, and he pressed on them lightly to make her sit down opposite him.

'Why don't you take a couple of weeks off and come with me for the first leg of my trip at least? We could spend some more time together. Aryan should be fine.'

But she was already shaking her head. 'I don't want to,' she said flatly.

Darius just didn't seem to understand, and she was done with trying to explain herself.

'I left Aryan for one night, and you saw what happened to him.'

'Yes—he had a breakthrough! Maybe the start of his recovery,' Darius countered.

Mallika clenched her teeth. He just wasn't getting it.

'If you want to spend more time with me, shouldn't

you stay here, instead of asking me to go with you? I have a perfectly good reason to want to stay here. Why should I leave my brother to traipse around after you just because you've got some quixotic notion in your head?'

Darius inhaled sharply as a whole lot of things suddenly fell into place for him.

'So *that's* the reason,' he said quietly. 'You're scared because I'm doing something that's a little unconventional and you don't know how to deal with it. All this stuff about not wanting to get into anything long-term is hogwash.'

'I'm not a risk-taker,' she said. 'So you're right—it bothers me. And if we're still in a relationship when you leave I'm not sure I'll be able to handle it.'

'Right,' he said, his expression tight and angry. 'So we stick to the original plan, then? It's over when I leave?'

'That would be best, I think,' she said.

She was so close to falling in love with him that she couldn't bear the thought of dragging out the end—pretending that they could sustain a long-distance relationship. There was only heartbreak at the end of it, but she couldn't bear to see him so upset either.

'Darius?' she said. 'I know you've tried to explain it many times, but *why* do you need to go?'

His expression relaxed a little and he said, 'I thought I *had* explained it. There's just so much more to life than this—so much to learn, so many places to explore, so many things to do... I don't want to wake up one day and discover that I've wasted most of my life. The world is such a big place, and I've only seen one small corner of it. I want to explore, have adventures, challenge myself—really see what I'm made of.'

'Right,' she said. 'I hear what you're saying, but I

guess my brain's just wired differently. I like the comfort of what's familiar…of doing what's expected of me.'

'It's wired just fine,' he said, reaching out to twine a lock of her hair around his fingers. 'I suppose I'm the one being unreasonable, asking you to stick with me when I'm not offering anything concrete in return.'

'It's not that,' Mallika said, and when he didn't reply, she added, 'I can't handle uncertainty, that's all. If it helps, I'm crazy about you.'

Darius's eyes darkened in response.

'How crazy?' he asked, and she pressed her body against his, nibbling at his throat and tugging his shirt out of his jeans to slide her hands over his hot bare skin.

'Moderately crazy,' she whispered. 'Actually, make that extremely crazy.'

He was moving against her now, lifting her so that her body fitted more snugly against his, and unbuttoning her top to get access to her pert, full breasts.

'I guess crazy will have to do for now,' he said, and she gasped as he finally got rid of her top and laid her down carefully on the nearest sofa. 'But I'm not going to give up on you.'

'I'll be moving out of the flat in a couple of days,' Darius said over lunch a few weeks later. 'The board's agreed to let me leave Nidas a little early.'

Mallika stared at him in dismay. While she was sticking to her decision, she hadn't realised how much it would hurt when he actually left. Unconsciously, she'd got addicted to him—to seeing him every day, hearing him laugh, running her hands over his skin and putting her lips to his incredibly sexy mouth.

Sometimes she thought that agreeing to go with him

for part of his trip would be worth the inevitable heart-ache—then all her old demons would came back to haunt her and she'd change her mind again.

'When are you leaving Mumbai?' she asked.

'Four weeks from now,' he said. 'But I thought I'd spend the last month or so with my parents and Shirin—just to make sure everything's settled for taking care of them while I'm away.'

Who's going to take care of me? Mallika felt like yelling at him, but she knew there was no point, so she tried to look as unconcerned as possible.

'Do you need help with moving?'

He hesitated. 'Not really. It's mainly clothes and some kitchen things—I'll be leaving most of it with Shirin anyway.'

'Finished packing?'

'No, I'll start tomorrow,' Darius said, wondering if he was being a colossal idiot.

He knew Mallika cared for him, and that if he pushed just a little harder he'd be able to break through her defences. But he'd planned for years to take this time off just for himself, with no work or family responsibilities, and he knew he'd regret it all his life if he stayed. And Mallika hadn't even *tried* to understand why he felt the way he did. If he stayed for her he knew he'd resent it—and her—after a while, and that would be the end of any kind of relationship.

He was halfway through packing the next day when the doorbell rang. Straightening up from the carton he was taping shut, he wiped a hand across his forehead. It was a hot day, and the number of cartons was growing alarmingly—he seemed to have collected a fair amount of junk in the few months that he'd lived in the flat.

'Oh, good, you're here,' Mallika said when he opened the door. 'I was worried you'd have already packed up and left.'

She was wearing skin-tight jeans and a peasant-style top that showed off her slender neck and shoulders, and Darius stood staring at her for a minute, his mouth growing dry with longing. Over the last few days he'd told himself over and over again that their relationship no longer made sense. He'd more or less bullied Mallika into giving it a shot, but now that his departure was imminent keeping the pressure on just wasn't fair. To either of them.

Wordlessly, he stood aside to let her into the flat. A whiff of her citrusy perfume teased his nostrils as she walked past and he bit his lip. Good resolutions were all very well, but he was only human.

Mallika stopped in the middle of the living room. 'Oh...' was all she said as she took in the cartons neatly lined up in rows and filling more than half the room.

'Shouldn't you have hired professional packers?' she asked. 'Do you have any help at all? Or are you trying to handle this on your own?'

'On my own,' he said. 'A lot of these are books and CDs—they take up more space than you'd think.'

But she wasn't listening to him any longer—her mouth was turning down at the corners and she put her arms around him abruptly, burying her face in his shoulder. 'I wish you didn't have to go,' she said, her voice muffled against his shirt. 'I'll miss you.'

'I'm leaving the country, not dying,' he said drily, though all he wanted to do was tip her face up and kiss her and kiss her, until there was no space for conversation or thought.

'Yes,' she said. 'But we won't have a place to be together for the next month. Unless....' She looked at him, her face lighting up. 'Oh, how silly—why didn't I think of it before? This flat'll be empty, won't it? I won't rent it out, and we can meet here whenever we want.'

Darius shut his eyes for a second. Mallika probably had no idea of what she was doing to him. All his life he'd prided himself on his decisiveness and self-control—it was only when he was with Mallika that he turned to putty.

'Don't leave India right away,' she said, stretching languorously on the bed a couple of hours later. 'Stay on in Mumbai for a few more weeks. You can start your self-discovery thing here just as well as in any other country.'

He shook his head, smiling at her. 'It won't work.'

She cuddled a little closer to him, pulling the sheet up to her chin. 'Don't move all your things, then,' she said. 'I'll cancel the lease agreement, so you won't need to pay rent, but you could come back to stay here whenever you want.'

Darius caught her close, pressing his lips to her forehead. 'Sweetheart, I need to do this *my* way,' he said. 'I need to work some things out, and I need a little space.'

The words stung far more than he'd meant them to, and he saw Mallika bite her lip to keep it steady.

'That's odd,' she managed finally, her tone as light as she could make it. 'I didn't have you pegged as someone who really got the concept of space.'

He gave her a wry grin. She had him there, and he

knew it. 'Perhaps you were right,' he said. 'Perhaps I never should have pressured you in the beginning.'

Mallika stared at him, a nasty, icy feeling gripping her heart. She'd been so close to telling him that she'd changed her mind—that she'd found she cared for him and wanted to give a long-distance relationship a shot. The last thing she'd expected was Darius himself having a change of heart.

'So you're saying that this is it?' she said, her voice still deceptively light. 'We don't stay in touch after today?'

'Something like that,' he said, and she nodded, not trusting herself to speak any more.

After a few seconds she slid out of bed, keeping the sheet wrapped around her as she collected her clothes from the floor.

'Be back in a minute,' she said, and slid into the bathroom.

For a few minutes she could only stare at her face in the mirror, feeling mildly surprised that it looked just as it usually did. Then, after splashing some water on her face, she quickly put on her clothes and flushed the toilet to account for the time she'd spent.

When she came out of the bathroom she looked as if she didn't a have a care in the world. Unfortunately Darius wasn't around to notice, and her lips trembled a little as she saw that he was already dressed and back to his packing.

'Got a lot to finish?' she asked, after watching him dump a big pile of clothes into a suitcase.

He shook his head. 'Another fifteen minutes or so. I'm sorry—I need to get this stuff done and then get back home. My mother has organised a family gathering and I promised I'd be there.'

She sat down on the bed, looking at him thoughtfully. One of the things *her* mother had repeatedly dinned into her head was to act with dignity. '*Apni izzat apne haath*— your dignity is in your own hands.' That had been one of her favourite sayings, along with, 'No one will respect you unless you respect yourself.'

'You should head off soon, then,' she said, getting to her feet with a brightly artificial smile on her lips.

It cost her every last ounce of willpower, but she walked across to him and leaned up to kiss him lightly on the lips.

'It was really good while it lasted,' she said. 'Thanks for putting up with all my whims and *nakhras*. Have a good life.'

'Mallika…' he said, and something indefinable flickered in his eyes.

She stepped back quickly, before he could touch her.

'I'll see you, then,' she said. 'Some time. Deposit the keys with the watchman, will you?'

And, leaving him standing in the bedroom, she hurried out of the flat, waiting till she was in her car before allowing a few hastily wiped away tears to escape.

CHAPTER ELEVEN

'I'M GOING OUT,' Aryan said.

He sounded oddly defiant—as if he expected Mallika to object.

It was almost a month since she'd broken up with Darius, and it had been tough. She missed him so badly that it hurt, and only the highest levels of self-control had stopped her from calling him.

Aryan hadn't said anything, but he'd been unusually well-behaved—probably sensing that she was very close to breaking point.

'Out?' she asked. 'Where?'

'Um…I thought I'd get a haircut. And maybe buy a couple of shirts.'

She should have felt pleased—Aryan was a lot better, but except for his trips to the doctor he'd stepped out of doors only once, for a walk around the garden with her. Wanting to go somewhere on his own was a first. He still ordered his clothes on the internet, and paid a local barber to come to their home and trim his hair once a month, and she couldn't figure out what had prompted the sudden decision to go to the shops on his own.

'D'you need the car?' she asked, trying to stall for time while she gauged his mood.

Aryan shook his head. 'Not today,' he said. 'I'll walk down Warden Road and get what I need. But if you could spare it for some time on Saturday that would be great?'

Feeling completely at sea, Mallika nodded. 'Yes, of course. You can have it for the full day, if you like.'

'I'm meeting someone,' Aryan volunteered after a brief silence. 'A...um...a girl. She's from Bangalore, and she's going to be here for a few days. I got to know her online,' he added a tad defensively as Mallika gaped at him.

'Figures,' Mallika muttered, once she'd got her breath back.

While she'd been obsessing about her little brother's lack of social interaction he'd gone right ahead and acquired an online girlfriend. Served her right for being so presumptuous, thinking he needed her help to get back to a normal life.

An unpleasant thought struck her, and she said, 'Aryan...?'

'Yes?'

'This girl—just checking—she's real, right? Not computer-generated or a...a...fake persona or something?'

Aryan laughed—a full-bodied, boyish laugh that made him look years younger. 'She's real, all right,' he said. 'I've video called her a few times, and I've done basic checks on her online profile. She's a computer engineer, and she's training to be a hacker. An *ethical* hacker,' he added hastily as Mallika choked on her tea. 'She's hired by corporates and governments to identify possible security breaches in their systems.'

'She sounds lovely,' Mallika said, wondering what kind of 'basic checks' one did on a prospective girlfriend. Finishing her tea, she got to her feet. 'Are you inviting her home?'

'I might,' Aryan said cautiously.

Mallika knew she had been a bit on edge ever since she'd broken up with Darius and Aryan was probably testing her mood. She turned her back to him now, and rinsed her tea cup with unnecessary vigour.

'You okay with me meeting her?' he asked.

'Yes, of course,' Mallika said, turning towards him with an overly bright smile on her lips. 'It's a good thing—you getting to know more people.'

She kept the smile plastered on her face until he left the flat, and then let out a huge sigh and flopped down onto the nearest sofa.

It was a relief, having the place all to herself to be miserable in. Aryan wasn't an intrusive presence, but he was around all the time, and sometimes she wanted to give full rein to her misery. Maybe scream and throw a few things, dignity be damned. She'd thought of going to the flat that Darius had vacated, being by herself for a few days, but it was too closely linked to him.

She'd gone back once, to get it cleaned and cover up the furniture, and the first thing she'd seen on walking in was the huge painting of a spice market that Darius had bought. He hadn't taken it with him, and it was still occupying pride of place on the living room wall. Walking closer to it, she'd noticed a little note stuck to the frame. *'Leaving this for you,'* it had said. *'Love, Darius.'*

It was the *'Love, Darius'* that had done it—she'd burst into tears, standing right there in front of the painting, and the skilfully etched heaps of nutmeg and chillies and cardamom had blurred into random blotches of colour.

Once she'd stopped sobbing she'd locked up the flat and never gone back.

Sighing, Mallika buried her face in her hands. She'd finally admitted to herself that she loved Darius, and that letting him go had been one of the stupidest things she'd ever done. She should have worked harder at their relationship instead of endlessly obsessing about her own troubles. But it was too late now—Darius had made it quite clear that he wanted a clean break.

After a while she pulled herself together and went out for a jog in a park near the sea. It had been a while since she'd last run, and she found the rhythm soothing—the steady pounding of her feet on the track helping her push everything to the back of her mind at least for a little while.

She stopped only when she was completely exhausted and the sun had begun to set. And when she got home she was so tired that she flopped into bed and sank into a blessedly dreamless sleep.

'It's the *annual party*!' Venkat said, in much the same tones that an ardent royalist might say, *It's the coronation*!

Strongly tempted to say *So...?* Mallika raised her eyebrows.

'You can't *not* come,' he said, looking outraged. '*Everyone* will be there.' He brightened up at a sudden thought. 'Darius will be there—he's still in town, and he's made an exception. We haven't told him, but we're holding a little surprise farewell for him at the end.'

Which was exactly the reason why she didn't want to go—but she could hardly tell Venkat that.

'I'll come,' she said. 'But I'll need to leave early. I have some relatives over.'

Well, Aryan *was* a relative, so technically she wasn't lying. And she could think of several things she would rather be doing that evening.

As it turned out, Darius was the first person she ran into when she walked into the party. *Of course*, she thought, giving herself a swift mental kick. She should have landed up there after nine, when the party would have been in full swing, said hello to Venkat and slipped out. Now she was terribly visible among the twenty or so people dotting the ballroom.

Darius found himself unable to take his eyes off Mallika. She was simply, even conservatively dressed, in a full-sleeved grey top and flared palazzo pants. The top, however, clung lovingly to her curves—and it didn't help that he knew exactly what was under it.

'Looking good,' he said, and her lips curved into a tiny smile.

'Thank you,' she said primly, hating the way her heart was pounding in her chest.

The people around them had melted away as soon as they saw Darius and Mallika together—even a blind man would have sensed the strong undercurrents to their conversation.

'Not too bad yourself,' Mallika added, just to prove that she wasn't shaken by his proximity.

It was true—in jeans and a casual jacket worn over a midnight-blue shirt Darius was breathtakingly gorgeous. His hair was brushed straight back from his forehead, and his hooded eyes and hawk-like features gave him a slightly predatory look. He'd lost weight in the last month, and his perfectly sculpted cheekbones stood out a little.

'Venkat said you mightn't come,' he said.

She shrugged. 'I don't like formal parties,' she said. 'But he made a bit of a point about it. So I thought I'd hang around until a quarter past eight and then push off.'

Darius glanced at his watch—it was barely eight, and most of the Nidas staff hadn't even arrived yet. In previous years the party had continued till three in the morning. While a few people had left earlier, even then, an eight-fifteen exit would set a new record.

'Do you really need to leave?' he asked. 'Dinner won't be served before ten.'

'I'll eat at home,' she said, giving him a quick smile. 'I'm not too keen on hotel food in any case.'

There was a brief pause, and then they both started speaking together. Somehow that broke the awkwardness, and when Darius laughed Mallika smiled back at him.

'You go first,' he offered.

'I was just asking how your parents are,' she said. 'And Shirin and the kids.'

'They're fine,' Darius said. 'Though my mum's taken to bursting into tears every time we talk about me leaving. It's driving my dad nuts.' His smile was indulgent, as if he was talking about a child and not a sixty-year-old woman. 'And Shirin's doing well. Her divorce hasn't come through yet, but we're hoping it'll happen by the end of the year. She's coping, the kids have settled and she's started looking for a job.'

'That's all good news, then,' Mallika said, smiling warmly at him.

He felt his heart do a sudden flip-flop in his chest.

'Yes,' he said stiltedly. It was tough enough, having to pretend that she was just like any other colleague. Having to actually stand here and carry on a superficial conversation was proving to be incredibly difficult.

'I'll…um…circulate a bit, then,' she said, indicating the half-full room. 'Now that I'm here I should say hello to as many people as I can before slipping out.'

He nodded, about to tell her that he'd like to see her before she left when the lights went out quite suddenly. A loud popping sound followed by the smell of burning plastic indicated a short-circuit.

Mallika stopped in her tracks as people around her gasped and exclaimed. A few women giggled nervously and Darius came to stand next to her, his features barely discernible in the dim light.

He took her arm and swivelled her around a little. 'Maybe you should wait till the lights are back on before you walk around and talk to people.'

'No, I'll just go now,' she said. She hated the dark, and the people milling around were making her nervous. 'I have a torch on my cell phone—hang on, let me put it on.'

The light from the torch was surprisingly strong, and he could see her quite clearly now, her brow furrowed in thought.

'Damn,' she said. 'This thing's running out of charge. I must have taken dozens of calls during the day, and I forgot to charge it before I left.'

'I'll walk you to the exit,' Darius said, taking her arm.

She thought of protesting, but her whole body seemed to turn nerveless at his touch—following him obediently seemed to be the sensible option.

'Shouldn't they put on a back-up generator or something?'

'They won't if it's a short-circuit,' he said. 'There's a risk of fire. Here—I think this is a shorter way out.'

He led her down a corridor that to Mallika looked exactly like the one she'd been in earlier. This was deserted, though, and it opened into a little *faux* Mughal courtyard with a small fountain in the centre. The fountain wasn't playing, but the pool of water around it shimmered in the faint light coming from the streetlights outside the hotel.

At that point the light coming from her phone flickered and the battery died. Mallika made a frustrated sound and shoved it into her bag. 'I can't call my driver now,' she said.

'D'you want to use my phone?'

'That would be very helpful,' she said drily. 'If only I remembered his number.'

'We'll page the car, then,' he said. 'Do you remember the car's number?

'Sort of,' she said. 'It has a nine and a one in it.'

'That helps,' he said gravely. 'Driver's name?'

'Bablu,' she said, so triumphantly that he laughed.

'We can page Bablu, then,' he said. 'That's assuming the paging system is working.'

She grimaced. 'I didn't think of that,' she said. 'Which way's the exit, anyway?'

He pointed to some glass doors opposite the ones they'd used to enter the courtyard.

'That way,' he said. 'Though we might as well sit here for a while. There's a bench over there, and it'll more pleasant outside than inside the hotel with no air-conditioning.'

She followed him to the bench, and he brushed a few leaves off it before they sat down. 'It's so quiet here,' she said. 'You'd hardly think we were in the middle of Mumbai.'

'The walls cut off the noise,' he said. 'But you can tell you're in Mumbai, all right. Look up—you can't see a single star because of the pollution.'

Mallika laughed. 'You're right, I can't,' she said. 'I should have known you'd burst my little fantasy.'

Darius went very still next to her. 'Why d'you say that?' he asked finally.

She flushed, thankful he couldn't see her in the dark. The words had slipped out, but she *had* been thinking of the happy bubble she'd been living in when they were still dating.

'It was just a stray remark,' she said, wishing he wasn't so perceptive. 'I didn't mean anything by it.'

'I think you did.'

'And I'm telling you I didn't!' Her voice rose slightly. 'Can't you just leave things alone, instead of digging around and trying to make me say more than I want to?'

'I'm sorry,' he said quietly, putting a hand over hers. 'I'm not trying to upset you.'

Mallika jerked her hand away. It was a childish gesture, but she was very near tears, and soon a few drops did escape and roll down her cheeks. She didn't wipe them off, hoping he wouldn't notice in the dark.

Of course she should have known better—Darius immediately leaned closer.

'Are you crying?' he asked, sounding so worried and concerned that her tears rolled faster.

'Of course not,' she said, trying to sound dignified and totally in control.

Unfortunately a little sniffle escaped, and Darius muttered something violent under his breath and swept her abruptly into his arms.

'Mallika—don't,' he said, trying to kiss the tears off her cheeks while simultaneously smoothing her curls away from her face. 'What's wrong? Is it something I did?'

Mallika fought for control and jerked away from him finally, scrubbing at her cheeks with her hands.

'It's all right,' she said. 'Moment of weakness. All better now.' She was feeling hideously embarrassed—crying all over an ex-boyfriend was the ultimate dumped woman cliché.

'It's *not* all right,' he said firmly. 'I know we're not together now, but I care about you still, and I'm not going away until you explain what's wrong.'

'*What* did you say?' Mallika asked, so stunned that she could hardly get the words out coherently.

'I'm not going away until I find out why you were crying,' he said.

'Before that, you dimwit!'

'We're not together now?'

'No, no—*after* that!' Mallika said, sounding outraged.

'I care about you still?' he asked, puzzled and amused in equal parts now.

'Yes, that's it,' she said, relieved that he'd finally got it right. 'Did you mean it?'

'Yes,' he said slowly. 'But you already know that.'

'You never told me!' Mallika said through gritted teeth. 'How the *hell* was I supposed to know?'

It was still dark, and Darius couldn't see her face, but he could sense the anger coming off her in waves. For the first time since he'd met her that evening he began to think that there might be some hope after all.

'Why else do you think I kept on trying to make it work for us?' he asked gently. 'Even when you kept sending me away?'

'I don't know!' she said. 'I thought it was general cussedness or something! And you lost interest as soon as your travel visas came in!'

He should have been annoyed at that, but right now what she was *not* saying was more important than what she was.

'I *do* care,' he said gently. 'In fact, I think I've been in love with you for a while now—only I kept trying to make myself believe that I was confusing attraction and affection with love. It was only after we split up that I realised how much I love you, and by then it was too late to do anything about it.

'You utter *idiot*,' she breathed.

He frowned. 'Does that mean...?'

'Of course it does,' she said, grabbing him by the shoulders and managing to shake him in spite of his bulk. 'I've been in love with you ever since you took me to meet your family that day. But after that you started to back off, and I didn't know what to think! I wanted to—'

What she'd wanted was lost as his arms came around her, crushing her against his chest.

'I've missed you,' he said, his lips hot and urgent against hers. 'God, so much.'

Mallika kissed him back just as hungrily, her hands gripping his shoulders as if she'd never let him go again. It felt so *right*, being back in his arms—she felt completely alive for the first time since he'd left.

'I missed you too,' she said, when she was able to speak. 'I'd think of calling you every single day, and then I wouldn't because I didn't want to seem desperate.'

'You couldn't have been more desperate than me,' he said wryly. 'I've been an idiot, Mallika. I was so sure I was doing the right thing.'

'By breaking up with me?' She shook her head, sounding confused. 'If you were in love with me, how could it possibly be the right thing?'

'I didn't know you cared for me too,' he said, tracing the delicate line of her jaw with one finger. 'It felt like I was forcing myself on you sometimes. Not physically,' he added as she made a sudden movement of protest. 'But you wanted to keep things light—and there I was, talking about long-distance relationships and making it work, when you clearly didn't want to listen... And you were obviously so uncomfortable with me giving up my job and leaving Mumbai that I thought the best thing to do would be to call a halt.'

'I've thought a lot about that,' Mallika said, sliding a hand up his chest to rest right against his heart. 'I think I finally do understand why you want to get away from the rat race—why you need to break away from what's expected of you.'

'So will you come with me?' he asked, capturing her hand in both of his and dipping his head to kiss it. 'At least for a while?'

The hidden lighting in the courtyard came on as if on cue, and he could see that her lovely lips were curled up slightly in a smile.

'I'd love to,' she said. 'Not right away—you should have the first few months to yourself, to do what you originally planned, and Aryan still needs me around—but I'll spend every bit of leave I get with you. And once you're back we can figure out what we should do.'

'Get married,' Darius said, and when she instinctively

pulled back he didn't let her go. 'I know all the reasons you have for not marrying,' he said. 'But if you think about it none of them hold if we're in love with each other.'

'I'm scared of marriage,' she admitted. 'Scared that things will go wrong and we'll end up being unhappy like my parents were. Even if we love each other now.'

'We'll be fine,' Darius said. 'Trust me.'

And suddenly Mallika knew that she did. She trusted Darius completely and absolutely, and she wanted to spend the rest of her life with him. Marriage still scared her, but she'd have plenty of time to get used to the idea.

'I love you,' she said softly. 'And you're right. We can make it work. Together.'

EPILOGUE

'*A GHAR JAMAI*—that's what these Hindustanis call men who marry their girls and move in with them,' Aunt Freny said with relish. 'That's what you're going to be. Not that we're not happy you're back. This gypsy-type living for a year might have been fun for you, but it drove all of us mad with worry. Hopefully once you marry you'll stay put. And as you've had your honeymoon before the wedding…'

'Freny!' Mrs Mistry said in awful tones.

Darius had been back for a month, tanned and leaner than he'd been when he left, but otherwise unchanged. Mallika had left Nidas and spent the last three months with him, travelling around Europe. After the wedding they would move into Mallika's flat in Parel, and then they had plans to set up a small company to aid NGOs with improving the infrastructure in rural areas.

'We're still going for a honeymoon, Aunt Freny,' Darius said mildly. 'It's just that it'll be in the villages around Mumbai.'

'It's his wedding day—you leave him alone, Freny,' Mrs Mistry said warningly as Freny geared up to retort. 'Come here, *dikra*, your collar's just a little crooked.'

Darius ignored her. 'Mallika's here,' he said, his eyes lighting up.

Aunt Freny snorted. 'Your son's a son until he gets a wife, et cetera, et cetera,' she said to Mrs Mistry. 'Though in your case your daughter really does seem set to be with you all her life!'

Luckily Mrs Mistry wasn't paying attention either, and she didn't hear Aunt Freny.

Mallika was walking in on Aryan's arm, dressed in a perfectly lovely red brocade sari with a heavily embroidered deep-red veil draped over her head. Her arms were loaded with gold bangles, and she wore a heavy gold *kundan* necklace around her slender neck. For the first time in years her curly hair was parted in the middle and tied back in a demure chignon, and she wore a red *bindi* in the centre of her forehead.

Darius was still gazing at her, spellbound, when she stumbled a little. She was quite close to him now, and he caught her by the shoulders to steady her.

'High heels,' she said, making a little face and laughing up at him. 'My aunt insisted.'

'You look lovely,' he said, meaning it.

She blushed a little. 'I don't feel like myself,' she said. 'If I could, I'd get married in my work clothes.'

'You'd look just as lovely,' he said, bending down to kiss her.

There was a collective indrawn breath from Mallika's side of the family, while Darius's smiled indulgently.

'Come on—let's get this show on the road,' Aryan said. 'Stop looking into each other's eyes, people.' His newly acquired, now *off*line girlfriend elbowed him, and he said, 'What? They'll miss the *muhurat* and Auntie Sarita will have a fit!'

It was a simple registered wedding, in spite of Mallika's interfering aunt's insistence on a traditional wedding sari and the actual signing happening at an auspicious time. Once they were done, both bride and groom heaved a sigh of relief.

'Any chance of us being allowed to skip the reception?' Darius asked hopefully.

His mother glared at him. 'Absolutely not,' she said firmly. 'How can you even suggest it, Darius?'

'Because I want to be alone with my wife,' he said in an undertone.

Mallika smiled up at him. 'We have the rest of our lives together,' she said, and he smiled back, putting an arm around her and pressing his lips to the top of her head.

'So we do,' he said softly as she slipped an arm around his waist and leaned in closer. 'Did I happen to mention how much I love you, Mrs Mistry?'

'You did say something about it,' Mallika said thoughtfully. 'But it wasn't all that clear. Could you explain it a little more clearly, please?'

* * * * *

Mills & Boon® Hardback
December 2014

ROMANCE

Taken Over by the Billionaire	Miranda Lee
Christmas in Da Conti's Bed	Sharon Kendrick
His for Revenge	Caitlin Crews
A Rule Worth Breaking	Maggie Cox
What The Greek Wants Most	Maya Blake
The Magnate's Manifesto	Jennifer Hayward
To Claim His Heir by Christmas	Victoria Parker
Heiress's Defiance	Lynn Raye Harris
Nine Month Countdown	Leah Ashton
Bridesmaid with Attitude	Christy McKellen
An Offer She Can't Refuse	Shoma Narayanan
Breaking the Boss's Rules	Nina Milne
Snowbound Surprise for the Billionaire	Michelle Douglas
Christmas Where They Belong	Marion Lennox
Meet Me Under the Mistletoe	Cara Colter
A Diamond in Her Stocking	Kandy Shepherd
Falling for Dr December	Susanne Hampton
Snowbound with the Surgeon	Annie Claydon

MEDICAL

Midwife's Christmas Proposal	Fiona McArthur
Midwife's Mistletoe Baby	Fiona McArthur
A Baby on Her Christmas List	Louisa George
A Family This Christmas	Sue MacKay

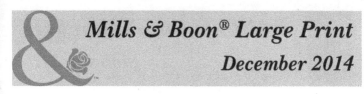

ROMANCE

Zarif's Convenient Queen	Lynne Graham
Uncovering Her Nine Month Secret	Jennie Lucas
His Forbidden Diamond	Susan Stephens
Undone by the Sultan's Touch	Caitlin Crews
The Argentinian's Demand	Cathy Williams
Taming the Notorious Sicilian	Michelle Smart
The Ultimate Seduction	Dani Collins
The Rebel and the Heiress	Michelle Douglas
Not Just a Convenient Marriage	Lucy Gordon
A Groom Worth Waiting For	Sophie Pembroke
Crown Prince, Pregnant Bride	Kate Hardy

HISTORICAL

Beguiled by Her Betrayer	Louise Allen
The Rake's Ruined Lady	Mary Brendan
The Viscount's Frozen Heart	Elizabeth Beacon
Mary and the Marquis	Janice Preston
Templar Knight, Forbidden Bride	Lynna Banning

MEDICAL

200 Harley Street: The Soldier Prince	Kate Hardy
200 Harley Street: The Enigmatic Surgeon	Annie Claydon
A Father for Her Baby	Sue MacKay
The Midwife's Son	Sue MacKay
Back in Her Husband's Arms	Susanne Hampton
Wedding at Sunday Creek	Leah Martyn

Mills & Boon® Hardback
January 2015

ROMANCE

The Secret His Mistress Carried	Lynne Graham
Nine Months to Redeem Him	Jennie Lucas
Fonseca's Fury	Abby Green
The Russian's Ultimatum	Michelle Smart
To Sin with the Tycoon	Cathy Williams
The Last Heir of Monterrato	Andie Brock
Inherited by Her Enemy	Sara Craven
Sheikh's Desert Duty	Maisey Yates
The Honeymoon Arrangement	Joss Wood
Who's Calling the Shots?	Jennifer Rae
The Scandal Behind the Wedding	Bella Frances
The Bridegroom Wishlist	Tanya Wright
Taming the French Tycoon	Rebecca Winters
His Very Convenient Bride	Sophie Pembroke
The Heir's Unexpected Return	Jackie Braun
The Prince She Never Forgot	Scarlet Wilson
A Child to Bind Them	Lucy Clark
The Baby That Changed Her Life	Louisa Heaton

MEDICAL

How to Find a Man in Five Dates	Tina Beckett
Breaking Her No-Dating Rule	Amalie Berlin
It Happened One Night Shift	Amy Andrews
Tamed by Her Army Doc's Touch	Lucy Ryder

Mills & Boon® Large Print
January 2015

ROMANCE

The Housekeeper's Awakening	Sharon Kendrick
More Precious than a Crown	Carol Marinelli
Captured by the Sheikh	Kate Hewitt
A Night in the Prince's Bed	Chantelle Shaw
Damaso Claims His Heir	Annie West
Changing Constantinou's Game	Jennifer Hayward
The Ultimate Revenge	Victoria Parker
Interview with a Tycoon	Cara Colter
Her Boss by Arrangement	Teresa Carpenter
In Her Rival's Arms	Alison Roberts
Frozen Heart, Melting Kiss	Ellie Darkins

HISTORICAL

Lord Havelock's List	Annie Burrows
The Gentleman Rogue	Margaret McPhee
Never Trust a Rebel	Sarah Mallory
Saved by the Viking Warrior	Michelle Styles
The Pirate Hunter	Laura Martin

MEDICAL

200 Harley Street: The Shameless Maverick	Louisa George
200 Harley Street: The Tortured Hero	Amy Andrews
A Home for the Hot-Shot Doc	Dianne Drake
A Doctor's Confession	Dianne Drake
The Accidental Daddy	Meredith Webber
Pregnant with the Soldier's Son	Amy Ruttan

MILLS & BOON®

Why shop at millsandboon.co.uk?

Each year, thousands of romance readers find their perfect read at millsandboon.co.uk. That's because we're passionate about bringing you the very best romantic fiction. Here are some of the advantages of shopping at www.millsandboon.co.uk:

✳ **Get new books first**—you'll be able to buy your favourite books one month before they hit the shops

✳ **Get exclusive discounts**—you'll also be able to buy our specially created monthly collections, with up to 50% off the RRP

✳ **Find your favourite authors**—latest news, interviews and new releases for all your favourite authors and series on our website, plus ideas for what to try next

✳ **Join in**—once you've bought your favourite books, don't forget to register with us to rate, review and join in the discussions

Visit **www.millsandboon.co.uk**
for all this and more today!